"There's only...you."

All of the moisture seemed to dry up in her mouth. Her gaze slowly slid over him. The last time she'd seen him had been months ago. She'd wanted to talk with him then, but her brothers had been determined to keep her away from him.

Her brothers were keeping secrets from her.

Only fair, really, because she'd been keeping plenty of secrets from them, too.

Mark was a handsome man. Powerful and commanding. He had high, slanting cheeks, a long, hard blade of a nose and lips that were...sexy. Sensual. She'd spent far too much time thinking about Mark's lips over the years.

"What the hell are you doing here, Ava? I thought you were staying away."

Not from him, but from Austin. From the McGuire ranch, because that place held too many painful memories for her.

But when no place seemed safe, where were you supposed to go?

SUSPICIONS

New York Times Bestselling Author

CYNTHIA EDEN

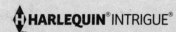

This book is for all of the wonderful Harlequin Intrigue fans
out there—thank you so much for your support!

ISBN-13: 978-0-373-69855-4

Suspicions

Copyright © 2015 by Cindy Roussos

Recycling programs
for this product may
not exist in your area.

Cynthia Eden, a *New York Times* bestselling author, writes tales of romantic suspense and paranormal romance. Her books have received starred reviews from *Publishers Weekly*, and she has received a RITA® Award nomination for best romantic suspense novel. Cynthia lives in the Deep South, loves horror movies and has an addiction to chocolate. More information about Cynthia may be found at cynthiaeden.com, or you can follow her on Twitter, @cynthiaeden.

Books by Cynthia Eden

Harlequin Intrigue

The Battling McGuire Boys

Confessions
Secrets
Suspicions

Shadow Agents

Alpha One
Guardian Ranger
Sharpshooter
Glitter and Gunfire

Shadow Agents: Guts and Glory

Undercover Captor
The Girl Next Door
Evidence of Passion
Way of the Shadows

Visit the Author Profile page at
Harlequin.com for more titles.

CAST OF CHARACTERS

Ava McGuire—Years ago, Ava survived a nightmare. She's been haunted by that brutal night ever since. And now, with her deadly past catching up to her once more, she knows that her life is on the line. Desperate, she turns to the man who saved her before—Mark Montgomery. If anyone can help her, she knows it will be him.

Mark Montgomery—Mark has lived next to the powerful McGuire family for years...and he has spent too many of those years fantasizing about the lovely Ava. He is tired of waiting in the shadows for her. And when danger strikes, he vows to do anything necessary to protect the one woman he can't let go.

Ty Watts—Ty is Mark's ranch foreman and longtime friend. He knows all about the pain in the McGuire family's past. When Mark gets involved with Ava, Ty knows that his friend is about to find even more danger heading his way. Ty also knows that he has to tread very carefully around the McGuires because he doesn't want them to learn his secrets.

Davis McGuire—When it comes to Ava's older brothers, the most protective one in the pack is Davis. An ex-SEAL, Davis never backs down from any challenge. Once upon a time, Davis and Mark were best friends, but then Davis realized that his *friend* was in love with Ava. Davis knows just how dangerous Mark truly is, and he doesn't trust the guy, not around his sister.

Alan Channing—Ava's former boyfriend. Alan isn't the boy that she remembers. He's grown up and become a powerful businessman. Alan has been working behind the scenes, manipulating other people so that he can get what he wants—and what he wants is for Ava to finally return home, where he thinks she truly belongs.

Prologue

"Help me!"

Her cry broke through the night, a long, loud, desperate scream.

Mark Montgomery had been standing on his front porch, staring up at the starry sky, but at that terrified call, he whirled around. At first he didn't see her. The darkness was too thick.

Thud. Thud. Thud. Thud.

He heard the unmistakable sound of a horse's hooves pounding across the ground. Someone was riding fast and hard, coming straight toward him.

He leapt off the porch.

"Help me!"

Her cry was even louder this time—and it was definitely a woman's voice. But there weren't any women at his ranch tonight. His mother had passed years ago, and there weren't any female ranch hands scheduled for a shift.

Then he saw the horse. It burst into the clearing near his house. The horse was a beautiful big black mare that he recognized—that was Lady. And Lady...Lady belonged to the McGuires, his neighbors who lived about ten miles away.

What the—?

A small figure was curled low on Lady's back, hugging the horse tightly. The horse's sides were shaking, its body wet with sweat after what must have been a brutal ride.

A ride in the middle of the night?

"M-Mark?"

And he knew that voice. Not screaming now, but soft, almost broken. He wanted to run toward that horse and rider, but he was afraid of spooking Lady, so he approached slowly, carefully. When the horse neighed, he reached out and softly touched Lady's mane. "It's okay." Then he reached up for the rider—Ava.

He could see her now. There was no mistaking Ava McGuire, not with that long, wild tumble of her hair. The moonlight and starlight spilled down onto her face, and the fear there made him lose his breath.

Some of his ranch hands had come into the yard, but they stayed a few feet back. "Get the horse!" Mark ordered as he pulled Ava off Lady.

She was like ice in his hands, and hard, heavy trembles kept raking her delicate frame. Ava had five brothers, all big, hulking military types, and Ava—the baby of the family—she was different. Delicate… Fragile… She was—

Crying. Because he'd just touched her cheeks and he could feel the wetness there. He wrapped his arms around her and held her tight. "What is it? What's happened?"

"Sh-shot…"

He could barely make out what she was saying.

"They…they were waiting…in the h-house…"

He caught her arms and eased back so that his gaze

could sweep over her. "Ava, did someone hurt you?" Rage pumped through him. Ava was only sixteen. If some jerks had hurt her, he would make them pay.

Her teeth were chattering. "Dead." She seemed to push out the word. "I'm scared. They're—dead."

Mark's whole body stiffened. "Who, Ava? Who are you talking about?"

She threw her body against his and started sobbing. "M-my parents! I saw them...the men...had guns! I heard the gunshots. I *ran*." Her sobs grew even harder. "I left them there..."

He held her as tightly as he could. There had to be a mistake. Her parents—they were fine, weren't they?

"Please," Ava begged him. "Help my parents. *Help them!*"

BUT THERE WAS nothing he could do. When Mark and his men went to the McGuire ranch, they didn't see the attackers. They just saw the blood.

Mark and his men made it to the ranch before the cops did. He was the first one in that place—and he would never forget the terrible sight that greeted him.

"Who would do something like this?" Ty Watts, Mark's ranch foreman, demanded as he stared at the brutal scene. "And *why*?"

There was no sign of the attackers. They were long gone. Mark stood there, the scent of blood heavy in the air around him, and he knew that he would be the one telling Ava that her parents hadn't survived.

He would be the one to give her the devastating news.

Mark bent down next to Ava's father. "I'm sorry," he whispered.

AVA STAYED AT his ranch for two days. During that time, she barely spoke. Her skin was too pale, her eyes far too wounded. She jumped at the slightest sound and during the night, she woke screaming. Again and again.

Mark didn't think he'd ever forget the sound of Ava's screams. He hated her pain and her grief, and he wished that he could do something to comfort her.

"I should have helped them." Ava's low voice had his head whipping toward her. They were on his porch, waiting, because Mark had gotten word that Ava's oldest brother had finally made it back to town. He'd learned of the slaughter at his family's ranch, and Grant McGuire had rushed home, flying back from some covert mission that had taken him to the other side of the world.

"Ava…" Mark sighed her name, and deliberately keeping his voice gentle, he told her, "The attackers had guns. What could you have done? You went for help!"

She shook her head, sending the dark locks sliding over her shoulder. "I left them to die."

She was breaking his heart. Ripping it right out with her quiet words.

"If you'd stayed," Mark forced himself to say, "then you'd be dead, too."

At first, Ava didn't speak. She stared down at her hands. Her fingers fisted. "I feel dead."

He strode toward her to pull her close. When she wouldn't look at him, he tipped back her chin. "Ava."

She flinched.

"You aren't dead." The thought of her dead—the thought of finding Ava… Ava with her slow smile and her warm green eyes…*dead*…that notion chilled him. "I won't let anyone hurt you."

He heard the sound of a car approaching. He didn't

let Ava go, but he glanced over his shoulder. Grant Mc-Guire had arrived. He'd come to take Ava away.

I don't want to let her go.

Because when Ava stayed with him at the ranch, he knew she was safe. He had his men on alert. They were patrolling constantly. But when Ava left…how was he supposed to watch out for her?

A car door slammed. Footsteps approached. But Ava was still staring up at Mark. He found that he couldn't look away from her.

"I'm scared," she whispered.

So am I. And very little scared him in this world.

"Ava!" That was Grant's voice. And suddenly Grant was charging up the steps. He pulled Ava into his arms and held her tight.

The guy's arms seemed to swallow Ava as she stood there, and Mark knew that Grant would be taking her away. The guy had flown halfway across the country in order to come home to Ava.

Grant turned toward him. "Thanks for watching my sister."

He forced his gaze to meet Grant's green stare. Green, like Ava's, but different. Colder. Harder. Fierce.

"I won't forget what you did." Grant shook Mark's hand. Then he looked back at Ava. "It's time to leave."

A tear slid down Ava's cheek, but she didn't make a sound. Mark's chest ached. He wanted to reach out to Ava and comfort her.

But Grant was the one to do that. Grant wiped away her tears before he pulled her close once again. "We're going to find the men who did this," he promised her. "They won't ever hurt anyone again."

And in that moment, Mark made a vow of his own.
No one would ever hurt Ava again.
Because her tears tore him apart.

Chapter One

Ava McGuire didn't have a lot of safe havens. And, outside of her family, there weren't exactly a lot of people she trusted.

In fact, only one person came to mind...

Mark Montgomery.

Ava slammed her car door and turned to the house. It was the middle of the night. *Not* the right time to be paying a visit to Mark's ranch, but she wasn't exactly overwhelmed with options.

I need to see him.

She straightened her shoulders and she marched toward his front door. She didn't let the memories swamp her as she climbed up the steps of the big wraparound porch. If she thought too much about the past, it would hurt. Those memories always did.

So she shoved the thoughts into the recesses of her mind, and she climbed those front steps. She reached for the doorbell but then the door opened.

Mark was there.

Tall, handsome, strong—*Mark*. His blond hair was tousled, and the light shone behind him, glinting off his shoulders. Very broad and bare shoulders because he wasn't wearing a shirt. Just a pair of low-slung jeans.

"Ava?" He reached out to her. As always, he seemed warm. His touch chased away the chill she'd felt since she'd first climbed into her car and begun the drive that would take her from her place in Houston to Mark's ranch in Austin. "What are you doing here?"

I needed to see you. I had to talk with someone...with someone who wouldn't think I was crazy.

Those words wanted to tumble out of her mouth, but she was trying to play things cool and not come across as the insane one. At least, not right away. She knew there were plenty of folks who already thought she was nuts or, much worse, a cold-blooded killer.

The rumors about her had persisted for years.

But...Mark had never seemed to believe those stories. He'd always stood by Ava and her family.

"I need your help," she told him quietly. She looked over his shoulder, hoping that no one else was there. The ranch house was huge, sprawling, but normally his staff stayed in separate quarters. She really didn't want anyone to overhear the confession she was about to make.

He pulled her into the house and shut the door behind her. "Ava, I'll give you anything you need."

Right. Because that was true-blue Mark. The guy who was always there to save the day. Or at least, that was the way she thought of him. Lately, though, her brothers had been acting differently when they spoke of Mark.

Her brothers had been friends with Mark for her whole life. And she, well, she'd been the tagalong. The little girl who bounced after the boys. *And who had always been in love with Mark Montgomery.*

Not that she'd ever told him that. Not him, not anyone. He kept his hand on her shoulder as they headed into his den. All of the lights were on in the place, and she saw a glass of wine sitting on the table.

Wine. No shirt...

Heat flooded her cheeks. "Do you have a…" *Not a lover, please, not a lover!* "Is someone here with you?"

One brow shot up. "Jealous?"

Wait, what? She shook her head. "I am so sorry. This—this was a mistake." What *had* she been thinking? She'd just been scared and she'd run. But she hadn't run back to her brothers because she couldn't handle going to the McGuire ranch or…having them stare at her with pity in their eyes as they wondered if she'd finally cracked under the pressure of their parents' murder.

Poor, fragile Ava…she just couldn't handle it anymore.

She pulled away from him, spun on her heel and marched for the door.

Mark stepped into her path. His arms crossed on that massive bare chest as he gazed at her. "I'm not letting you go now." The words seemed to hold the edge of a threat. Or a promise?

"Mark?"

"I waited too long," he murmured.

She backed up a step.

"No one else is here." His voice was flat. "There is no girl waiting in my bedroom—if that's what you're thinking. There's only…you."

All of the moisture seemed to dry up in her mouth. Her gaze slowly slid over him. The last time she'd seen him had been months ago. They'd been at the funeral of Austin police detective Shayne Townsend. She'd wanted to talk with Mark then, but her brothers had been determined to keep her away from him.

Her brothers were keeping secrets from her.

Only fair, really, because she'd been keeping plenty of secrets from them, too.

Mark was a handsome man, powerful and commanding. He had high, slanting cheeks, a long, hard blade of a nose and lips that were…sexy. Sensual. She'd spent far too much time thinking about Mark's lips over the years.

He was big, easily a few inches over six foot, with those strong, broad shoulders that he'd used back in his high school football days. His skin was a sun-kissed gold, his eyes a dark blue. When he looked at her with those eyes, Ava sometimes felt as if he could see *through* her.

But right then, Mark's eyes held confusion and worry.

"What are you doing here, Ava? I thought you were staying away."

Not from him, but from Austin and from the Mc-Guire ranch because that place held too many painful memories for her. But when no place seemed safe, where were you supposed to go?

He's my haven.

"Ava?"

"I'm not crazy."

"I never said you were." His hands dropped and he took a step toward her. "Never thought it, either."

Others had. How many times had she heard the whispers over the years?

Is that her? Did she do it?

They should have locked her up…

She's either crazy…or she's a killer.

Ava swallowed and lifted her chin. "Someone has

been in my house." The little one-bedroom cottage in Houston that she called home.

"What?" Now a lethal fury had entered his voice.

"He didn't take anything. Nothing was broken, so I couldn't really report it to the police. I just… I know someone has been inside." It was the small things that had tipped her off to the intruder's presence. Things that most people probably wouldn't have noticed.

A confused furrow appeared between Mark's brows. *He doesn't believe me.*

"Pictures have been moved." Now she spoke quickly, the words tumbling out as she tried to convince Mark that she was telling the truth. "Like someone picked them up, but put them back down in the wrong place."

His square jaw locked. He had a faint cleft in his chin. Something else that was sexy about him.

"That's not all," she hurried to say because she knew the picture thing sounded flimsy. "My clothes were re-arranged." She felt the heat stain her cheeks. "He went through my dresser and…touched things. Moved them." Her underwear. Her bras. He'd been in her closet, too. The clothes had been moved—pushed to either side just a few extra inches.

At first she'd thought she was imagining all of these small things. But…then they kept adding up. And she hadn't been able to shake the feeling that someone was watching her.

No, worse.

Stalking her.

Now Mark was just staring at her.

"I'm not imagining this," she whispered as she gazed up at him. "It's happening. When I got home this evening, it had happened again. My back door…

it was unlocked. He just left it unlocked when he left."

Mark was still staring. He had to believe her! "I *triple*-checked that door before I went out. I know it was locked, I *know*—"

His hands wrapped around her shoulders. "Why didn't you call the police?"

"I did...the first time. They came out, looked around and said there was no sign of any intruder." The police had basically told her to stop wasting their time...only in a nicer way.

"Your brothers," he snapped out the words. "They own a PI business, for goodness' sake! They'd be on this thing in an instant. They'd—"

"Lock me up and throw away the key." Her words were brittle. "You know my brothers and exactly what they're like." Military through and through, and when it came to her...about a million times too protective. "I don't want to go back to the McGuire ranch. You know that. I *never* want to stay there again." Because every time she went there, Ava hurt. "This is just a jerk playing some kind of sick game with me. I want the game to stop. I want—"

Mark was shaking his head and his hold on her tightened. "Breaking into your house isn't a game. It sounds like someone is fixated on you! Stalking you!"

That was what she feared.

"What if he escalates? What if he decides to break into the house while you're there?"

Just why did Mark think she'd driven all the way to Austin? That unlocked door had sent her into a tailspin, and she'd been horrified at the thought of staying in that place for even one more night. She'd already put plans in motion to leave Houston, but tonight's little fright fest had moved up her departure by a few days. "That's where you come in," she told him.

His face was just inches from hers.

"I need a place to stay." He hadn't seen her car yet. So he didn't know... "I was already planning to move to Austin... I was offered a job at the art museum. I was scheduled to start in two weeks, but I already turned in my notice at my old job, and..." And she was talking way too fast. "Whoever was messing with me in Houston, he won't follow me to Austin. It's a new city." That's what she'd been telling herself. "I'll get an apartment here and vanish."

"Ava..."

"Until I find that apartment, I need a place to stay." She licked her lips. His gaze immediately fell to her mouth. Was it her imagination or did his blue stare heat up? "Please, Mark, can you let me stay here just for a few days? Until I find a more permanent place?"

Because she'd always felt safe with him.

But his jaw seemed to lock down even harder. His breath heaved out and he—he backed away from her. "If someone is stalking you..." He took another step back. "You need to call your brothers. They're the experts at this kind of thing. They'll find the guy—"

"If they even believe someone was in my place." She wasn't so sure they'd buy her story. They treated her with kid gloves as it was, always trying to hide the truth about their investigation into their parents' death. They didn't get that she wasn't some scared teen any longer.

He frowned at that. "Of course they'll believe you."

He sounded so confident. The cops hadn't believed her. Her neighbors hadn't believed her. "Do you believe me?"

"Yes." He gave a grim nod. "And you should have come to me *immediately*. I mean, how long has the joker been doing this to you?"

"A month." He believed her. Relief swept through Ava, almost making her feel a little dizzy.

Fury darkened his face. "You wait this long to tell me? You only come to me when you're terrified. You don't—"

"I changed the locks. My brothers had installed a security system—a top of the line system. I tried to stay safe." *On my own.*

"You have to tell them."

"My brothers haven't exactly been living the easy life lately," she muttered. Grant had nearly died a while back when he was working a case. He'd wound up in the hospital. And as for Brodie—he and his girlfriend had both just battled a monster from their past. They'd barely made it out of that nightmare alive. "They've had enough to deal with, okay?"

"*You're their sister.* They'd drop everything for you."

She glanced away from him. "I just need a place to stay tonight, okay?" Did he want her to beg? Because she was close to it. She couldn't stay in a motel. The walls in places like that were thin. "It's too late to call them now." If he'd just let her stay the night, she could figure out another plan for tomorrow.

"Bull. You came to *me* this late. Their ranch is just down the road."

Her gaze fell to the floor. "I wanted to be with you." But now that seemed foolish. He sure hadn't greeted her with open arms. "I shouldn't have come." She turned away and started heading back toward the door.

"No, you can't leave."

And he was touching her again, spinning her around to face him. Staring at her with fury and—and some other dark, turbulent emotion shining in his eyes. "You come to me," Mark continued, "telling me that some bozo is stalking you…and you expect me to just watch as you walk away in the night?"

She swallowed. "No, I expect you to give me a room…for old time's sake." Tomorrow, when she wasn't dead tired from fear and exhaustion, she'd work on another plan. One that didn't involve her brothers totally flipping out.

He gave a curt nod. "You can stay as long as you want."

Yes! That relief was so strong that she was *definitely* feeling a little light-headed. Or maybe that was just because she hadn't eaten since breakfast. "Thank you." Impulsively she stood on her toes and wrapped her arms around him. His rich masculine scent filled her nose. "You've always been a good friend to me."

Mark's body was rock hard against hers—hard and hot and so incredibly strong. His hands settled along the curve of her hips. "Is that what I am?" His voice was deeper, almost a growl.

She lifted her head and stared into his eyes. "Yes." Her own voice came out too husky, so she cleared her throat and tried again. "Yes, but you're also…more."

"Am I?" His gaze had locked on her mouth.

Her heart thundered in her chest. "You're almost family."

"No." An instant denial. His hold urged her even closer to his body. "I'm not family. Don't ever think that I am." His eyes were still on her mouth. And his head was lowering toward hers, closing that last little bit of space. "I'm not your brother, and I'm not some safe friend."

She trembled against him. "Mark?"

His gaze slowly lifted and met hers. "You should be careful with me."

Her drumming heartbeat seemed to shake her chest. She'd never worried about being careful with Mark. Mark was good, solid and dependable. The light in the dark. He was—

"Because I'm not sure how much longer I can be careful with you."

He was going to kiss her. Ava was sure of it. Mark was so close to her, the tension in the air had turned blazing, and she wanted him to press his mouth to hers. She'd wondered if he would ever actually—

He backed away. Again.

She suddenly felt very cold.

"You know the guest room is down the hallway." He pointed to the left.

Yes, she knew where the guest room was.

Just as she knew that Mark's room was on the other side of the sprawling ranch house. Far enough away... *that he won't hear me scream.*

She thought about going out to the car for her bags, but figured she'd just save that for another time. Her car was parked near the entrance to Mark's house, and the bags would be safe there for the time being.

For now, she'd crash...because she needed to slip away from Mark and his too-watchful gaze.

She turned on her heel and headed for the hallway.

"Tomorrow," he called after her, "we call your brothers."

She reached out and touched the door frame. "They

don't want me near you." Not now. She didn't know what had happened, but she'd been given that warning by more than one McGuire. Ava looked back at Mark.

He hadn't moved.

Had he even heard her? Sighing, she took a step forward.

"What do you want, Ava?" His low, rumbling words stopped her.

And an instinctive response...*you*...rose to her lips. But she managed to choke that word back.

"Ava?"

"I don't want to be scared anymore," she said, and those words were the truth.

Or at least, as much of the truth as she was willing to share right then.

Ava kept walking, and Mark didn't say anything else.

AVA WAS BACK.

Mark glanced down at his hands. There was a faint tremble in his fingers. He almost hadn't been able to let Ava go. Not when her sweet lips were so close to his.

Once it had been easy to stay away from Ava. But... Ava wasn't some scared sixteen-year-old girl any longer. She'd grown up and transformed into the most beautiful woman he'd ever seen.

When Ava was near, he ached. Because he wanted... what he shouldn't have.

He sucked in a breath and could have sworn that he tasted her. The scent of strawberries seemed to cling to Ava. A light, sweet scent. She'd been in his arms, her body pressed tightly to his, and he'd wanted to devour her.

He'd also wanted to destroy whoever was out there

terrorizing her. Because Ava had been afraid. Her body had trembled, her breath had caught in her throat and her green eyes had been bright with fear. Some jerk had been stalking her for a month, and she was just *now* telling him about it?

He spun away. Grabbed up his glass of wine and downed the contents in one fast gulp.

First thing tomorrow he'd be calling her brothers. Once upon a time he and Davis McGuire had been best friends. There was no way he'd let Ava keep this dangerous secret from her family.

First thing tomorrow...

But for that night, Ava would rest. She'd be safe.

He started to pace. He'd keep watch over her now, same as he'd done years ago.

The night she'd first run to him was burned in his memory. How could a man forget a night of death? It was impossible, as impossible as forgetting a woman like Ava.

She'd grown up before his eyes. That terrible night had destroyed the last of her childhood. At first she'd been so brittle, so very breakable. He'd wanted to pummel anyone who looked at her too hard, and there had been plenty of accusatory stares. Sure, he'd heard the rumors.

Some folks thought it was suspicious that Ava had escaped from the killers without even a scratch while her parents had died.

He paced toward the window on the right. *Suspicious?* No, there was nothing suspicious about her survival. She'd been lucky. He had no doubt that if the killers had seen her, Ava would have died, too.

Years had passed since that night. Bubbly, happy

Ava had vanished. She'd become controlled, withdrawn and beautiful as she finished her college years. She'd gone to grad school, and she'd kept away from Austin.

But she's back now.

Back with him. In his home, but not in his bed. Though for the past two years, he'd sure imagined her there plenty. Ever since the night he'd tasted Ava for the first time. It had been a kiss that shouldn't have happened. A kiss that had changed everything for him.

His eyes squeezed closed. It was really going to be a long night.

AVA WAS IN the stables, stroking Lady's mane. She was humming a bit as she groomed her horse. Working kept her mind off the fact that she and her boyfriend Alan had broken up just hours before the homecoming dance. *Because he was a serious jerk with delusions.* And now she was there, alone with her horse, while all of her friends were out at the party.

Ava stopped humming. There would be other dances. And plenty of other guys—guys who weren't creeps and who—

Thunder cracked through the night. At the sound, Ava's whole body jerked. There wasn't supposed to be a storm that night. As the sharp crack died away, goose bumps rose on Ava's arms.

Was that thunder?

She whirled from the horse, ran from the stable. That loud blast still seemed to echo in her ears. As she ran, she looked up at the star-filled sky. There was no sign of clouds or lightning. Nothing at all.

Fear thickened in her veins. *Something is wrong. I don't think that was thunder.* She rushed toward the ranch house. All of the lights were blazing inside. She could see her dad standing a few feet in front of the picture window.

Only he wasn't alone.

Ava staggered to a stop. The lights were so bright in that house, and she could easily see the men with her father. Two men wearing black ski masks were pointing guns at her father.

Where's Mom? Where's Mom?

She inched closer, and when she saw her mother lying on the floor, a pool of blood gathering near her body, a sob tore from Ava. In that instant, her father whirled toward the window. His gaze locked with hers.

Dad!

"Run." He mouthed that one word at her.

Ava shook her head, too terrified to move.

But then her father whirled around to face the men in masks. He shouted something at them, words that drifted through the open window.

"I'll never tell you. No matter what you do. I'll never tell."

Boom! That time, she knew the sound wasn't thunder. She saw her father's body jerk. Ava watched in horror as he fell, and she was screaming, screaming—

"Wake up, Ava." Warm, strong hands wrapped around her shoulders and shook her once, gently. "It's okay. You're safe. I've got you."

Her eyes flew open. She saw that the lights were all on—and so bright—in that guest room. Mark was on the bed with her, his body curled protectively over hers.

"It's just a dream," he told her, his deep voice rumbling. "Dreams can't hurt you."

No, it was the men in black ski masks who did

that. Those were the men who appeared and wrecked your world.

Ever since that stalker had started playing games with her life a month ago, she'd been having the dreams—every single night. Before that, she'd been doing so much better. She'd even been able to go a few months without the nightmares.

But since the first time she'd noticed her pictures rearranged...it was as if the past had come rushing back to her.

His thumbs traced little soothing circles on her arms. "I didn't know you still—"

"Still woke up screaming." Her voice sounded raspy. How long had she been screaming before he'd rushed in? "That's why I could never have a roommate in college." Why she'd gotten the little rental house close to the campus. Her brothers had put in a security system there to keep her safe...and she'd really thought everything would be fine.

But someone still got in.

"The stalker, he brought it all back." She sat up in bed, but Mark didn't let her go. "I was getting better."

He didn't speak. His hands were so warm around her.

He'd come to her before, comforting her in the middle of the night. But she'd been a scared sixteen-year-old then.

She was still scared, but she wasn't sixteen.

And Mark...he wasn't leaving. Instead, he was watching her with an intense, turbulent gaze. She wished she could read his mind right then.

Wished—

His gaze fell to her body. She was wearing her bra and panties—she'd ditched everything else before she climbed into bed. Since his room was on the other side of the house, she'd hoped that he wouldn't hear her cries when the nightmare came.

He had.

His hands tightened on her. She could feel the calluses along the edge of his fingertips. Mark wasn't just some figurehead at the Montgomery ranch. He worked day in and day out. She knew he was the lifeblood of that place.

She also knew that she should feel embarrassed to be with him this way. She should probably reach out and pull up the covers. She didn't.

"Do you remember," Ava asked him, "when we kissed?"

Maybe he didn't remember. He'd been drinking that night. She had, too, or else she probably would never have gotten up the courage to kiss him. She'd just finished her undergraduate degree, and she'd been celebrating the holidays with her brothers—and with Mark. She and Mark had been alone for just a moment. The mistletoe had been right above them. She'd stood up on her toes and pressed a quick kiss to his lips.

Then something had happened. He'd taken over that kiss. It hadn't been quick. It had been deep and hot.

"I wish I could forget."

His words hurt, and she sucked in a sharp breath. "I—"

"Because if I could forget, then I wouldn't spend so much time wanting to taste you again." His right hand rose and sank into her hair, tipping back her head. "Like this…"

His lips pressed to hers softly at first, carefully.

But she didn't want careful. Not from him. Everyone else in her life treated her as if she'd break apart at any moment. *Not Mark, too.*

Her hands curled around his shoulders. Her mouth opened beneath his, and her tongue slid out to caress his lower lip.

His body stiffened, and she heard him groan. She loved that sound. Loved it even more when he stopped being so careful. She could feel his passion taking control. One minute he was holding her as if she were fine china, and the next he'd crushed her back into the bedding. He was on top of her, kissing her deep and hard, and she loved it.

For just a moment, the ghosts and fears from her past were gone. All she knew was the need she felt for Mark. The desire that was burning hot inside her, singeing her to her core. Her nails bit into his shoulders. Her breasts tightened, ached, and her nipples thrust against his bare chest.

Her hips were arching up. The covers were tangled around her legs, though, keeping her from feeling all of his body. She wanted those covers gone. She didn't want anything between them.

Her hands slid over his back. There were some scars there, faint ridges that rose beneath her fingers. She wondered how he'd gotten those marks, but then her hands kept moving because she wanted to explore every inch of him.

Ava knew plenty about nightmares. But because of Mark, she also knew a bit about dreams. And since he'd kissed her two years ago, she'd dreamed of being like this with him.

Only him.

His mouth pulled from hers and, for a moment,

she thought he was going to back away. He didn't. He started kissing a scorching path down her neck. She arched up against him as she moaned. She *loved* it when he kissed her at the base of her throat, and when he lightly sucked the skin, then scored it with his teeth... *"Mark!"*

"Want to taste all of you...everything..."

She wanted to taste all of him.

He was still moving down her body, only now he'd just jerked the covers out of the way. She thought she might have heard the sheet rip, but Ava couldn't be certain of that. Her mind was focused on other things.

On him.

On the way he made her feel.

On the desire that was making her body ache.

His fingers slid under the edge of her bra. "Stop me," he said.

Was he crazy? Stopping him was the last thing she wanted. "Touch me," Ava said instead.

Because she was looking at his eyes, she saw his control break away. Saw his pupils swell as the darkness swallowed the blue of his gaze. Then he was shoving her bra out of the way. His fingers curled over her breasts, stroked her nipples and a ragged gasp tore from her. Yes, yes, this was what she wanted.

No fear. No pity. Nothing but pleasure.

Mark.

Then his mouth was over her breast. "So pretty," he whispered before his lips closed over her nipple. He sucked her, laving her with his tongue, and Ava nearly went crazy. Her hips bucked because the feelings coursing through her body were too strong. She needed him, wanted him. This moment had finally come, *finally*.

She felt as if he'd been staying away from her since that kiss, and Ava had feared that she'd imagined his desire for her.

But I didn't. He wants me just as badly as I want him.

There was no stopping. His hands were sliding down her stomach now, heading for her panties. There was—

An alarm shrieked, blaring through the house. Mark's head whipped up. He stared at her for a moment and shook his head as if he were coming out of a fog. Then he bolted from the bed.

"Mark!"

"Stay here!" he said as he rushed for the door. "Something set off the alarm near the stables—I know that alarm!"

He was leaving her.

Her breath heaved out. White-hot passion one moment…fear the next. That would *not* be the story of her life. Ava jumped out of the bed. Her knees did tremble but she stiffened them up, and she grabbed for her clothes. One minute later, she was running out of that bedroom door and racing to keep up with Mark.

Because if she'd brought danger to Mark's ranch, there was no way she was letting him face it alone.

Chapter Two

Mark rushed out of his house, his bare feet flying over the wooden porch. The alarm was still blaring up ahead, a security measure he'd put in after a psychotic SOB had torched his stables a few months back. The jerk had been trying to get at Brodie McGuire and Brodie's girl, Jennifer, and the fire had been set to lure them both into a trap.

No one will use me again.

He could see some of his ranch hands already running toward the stables. There was no sign of a fire, but something had sure set off the alarm.

The whole ranch was wired with state-of-the-art security, courtesy, of course, of the McGuires. He'd been watching the security feed when he'd first seen Ava pull into his drive earlier that night. Ava already knew the code to get past his gate, and he'd watched her, stunned to see her back at *his* place. Especially since her brothers had told him to stay away from her.

"Ty!" He yelled for his foreman because he had just come from the back of the stables. "Are the animals all right?"

Ty Watts hurried toward him. "Looks clear, Boss." Ty was close to Mark's age, with dark hair and dark brown eyes. "I didn't see anyone out back, and the men are in there with the horses now."

But something had set off the alarm—something or someone.

"What the hell do you think...?" Ty began. Then he let out a low whistle. "Sorry. Didn't realize company was here." His gaze was directed over Mark's shoulder.

Mark glanced back and saw Ava. Her hair tumbled around her shoulders. Under the lights that had flashed on with the security system, she appeared even more beautiful as the harsh glare lit up her body.

She was running toward Mark, clearly coming from the house.

In the middle of the night.

"Like that, is it?" Ty murmured.

Mark cut him a killing glare. "Yes," he told him flatly. "It is."

"What's happening?" Ava asked, her voice husky as her breath heaved out. The woman even sounded like sin right then. He'd had her beneath him moments before. His hot dreams had been about to become reality, and then—

The alarm had been a cold shower. A hard wake-up that had stopped him from making a terrible mistake.

Would it have been a mistake? Or would it have been the start of an addiction I couldn't end?

"Something set off the sensors at the rear of the stables, ma'am," Ty told her, his Texas accent rolling beneath the words. "After the recent fire, Mark here didn't want to take any chances with the horses' safety. Those sensors go off if anyone gets too close during the night."

A few more ranch hands came out. "Clear!" one of them shouted.

"Could have just been some animal checking out the place. Maybe a raccoon," Ty said. "It could even have been a coyote."

Ava was staring straight at Mark. "Do you have cameras set up back there?"

"No, not there," he said. "Not yet, anyway. The cameras are all connected to the main house and to the main road that led to the ranch."

"What if I led someone here?" Ava asked as she stepped closer to Mark. "What if I did this?"

"Nothing happened," he told her flatly. "You didn't do anything." He nodded toward Ty. "Have the men search the grounds just in case. We don't want to leave anything to chance."

Ty nodded and turned away. A few seconds later, Mark heard Ty barking orders to his men. Mark wanted to go and join the search, too, but he needed to make sure Ava was safe. "I thought I told you stay inside," he said as he leaned in toward her.

"I don't always stay where I'm put." Her voice held a distinct edge. "If there was a threat out here, I didn't want you facing it alone."

Ava…riding to his rescue. And some folks thought she was weak? Those folks didn't know her at all. "I just wanted you safe."

She stared up at him. "Are any of us ever really safe?"

With her past, yes, she'd wonder that.

"I want to help, and I don't intend to help by hiding inside your house." She straightened her shoulders. "If you're searching, then I'm going with you."

"Ava…"

"I...can't wait in there alone." Her voice was stark. "Don't ask me to."

He understood. He offered his hand to her. "Stay with me every step?"

Her smile flashed. "Of course. That's how I keep you safe, right?"

She had a gorgeous smile. One that winked dimples on each side of her mouth. He hadn't seen that smile of hers in a long time. He'd missed it.

The same way he'd missed her.

Ava put her hand in his.

FROM HIS HIDING PLACE, he watched Ava McGuire and Mark Montgomery cross the paddock. Ava was making a huge mistake. She couldn't trust Mark, not for an instant. She needed to realize how dangerous he was to her.

Mark had been keeping secrets from Ava for years. He'd been lying to her. And now she was going to turn to the man for help? *Wrong move, Ava. Wrong.*

In fact, that move could prove deadly for her.

Ranch hands were scrambling around, checking on the horses, trying to make sure they were all safe. Mark stayed beside Ava every moment, but he didn't think it was because he wanted to protect her.

You just want her.

In many ways, Mark Montgomery was just like his old man. When he saw something that he wanted, he took it, not caring at all for the consequences. Or for the shattered lives that he left in his wake.

Mark wanted Ava, so he thought he'd take her.

That won't happen.

Ava wasn't going to be destroyed. The Montgomerys had already wrecked enough lives. Maybe it was time for Ava to learn the truth about her so-called hero.

He slipped back into the shadows.

Maybe it was time for everyone to learn the truth.

THEY SEARCHED THE PROPERTY but found no sign of an intruder. Mark headed back to the house with Ava by his side. She seemed tense next to him, and he knew she had to be exhausted. They'd spent at least an hour out there because—

Because I wanted to make sure the jerk who has been harassing Ava didn't follow her to my home.

He shut the door behind them and set the alarm. "You should try to get some sleep." He wasn't touching her right then. Probably a good thing because the more he touched, the more he wanted.

I had her in the bed beneath me. Her breast in my hand. In my mouth. She was moaning for me. Ava wanted me.

And he'd been about thirty seconds away from taking the woman he wanted most.

He turned away from her.

"You're not going to talk about it, are you?" Ava asked him.

He locked his jaw. "The alarm went off. Maybe it malfunctioned. Maybe someone was here. I don't—"

She grabbed his arm and pulled him around to face her. "I'm not talking about the alarm. I'm talking about us!"

He tried to unclench his back teeth. "There isn't an us." Even though he spent too much time thinking about her. Even though he wanted to strip her right then and get her back on a bed once more. Even though—

"Why not?" Ava asked. Her eyes were big. Her gaze so deep. "Don't you want me?"

Wanting her sure wasn't the problem. He cleared his throat. "The age...difference between us is—"

"Bull."

He blinked.

"So you're a bit older than me. I'm not some kid. I'm in my twenties. I've got a graduate degree. I support myself." She waved the age difference away. "My brothers have dated plenty of women who are older and younger than they are, so don't give me that baloney. We're both legal."

"Your brothers...they are my friends."

She exhaled. "Are you sure about that? Because Davis told me just a few months ago... He said you weren't the man I thought you were."

And Davis had been acting odd around him ever since Detective Shayne Townsend had died. Mark didn't know what was happening, but the McGuires had definitely put the freeze on him.

"But I don't really care what Davis thinks about you. *I* want you."

Then she leaned forward, trying to wrap her arms around him.

He stepped back.

Hurt flashed across her face.

"Ava..."

"You were kissing me like a desperate man earlier. Like you didn't need anything more than me in the whole world." She shook her head. "Now you back away from me? *Why?*"

"Because I don't want to hurt you."

A faint line appeared between her brows. "You

wouldn't! You never have. You're the one who has always been there for me. Never judging, just accepting. You know all of my secrets."

"But you don't know mine, Ava." And that was the problem. He'd shielded her from that part of his life. Did the very best that he could not to taint her image of him.

But Ava didn't know the things he'd done. Ava didn't know about the dark core inside of him and, for her sake, he hoped that she never did.

Ava had always looked at him as if he were some kind of hero. He wasn't. He was about as far from hero material as a man could get. If she knew the things he'd done, Ava would never let him so much as touch her again. *And that's why she won't ever know.*

"Go to sleep," he told her because he had to put some distance between them. He couldn't be that close to Ava and not feel her sensual pull. "It's been a long day." He walked away from her.

AVA STARED AFTER MARK, narrowing her eyes. He was seriously just walking away? She wanted to scream at the man. Finally, *finally*, they'd been close. The desire had been burning between them. There had been no barriers. Nothing at all holding them back, and now—

Now he was pulling away.

It won't be that easy, Mark.

She headed back toward the guest room. Sleep wasn't going to come for her, not then. Adrenaline spiked her blood, and if she slept—well, she wasn't in the mood to deal with a second nightmare. No way.

Ava pushed open the door to her room. It was dark inside. Pitch black.

Ava hesitated. She'd been sure that she left the lights on when she ran out earlier. The lights had been blazing. She'd dressed as fast as she could and then rushed out after Mark.

And I didn't turn the lights off.

She glanced back over her shoulder. "Mark?"

It was just like before. Small things. Things that most people would overlook. But after a while, those little things had started to add up.

Ava pulled in a deep breath. Then her hand slid out, moving along the wall near the door. Her fingers touched the light switch. She flipped it on, fast, and illumination flooded the room.

The bed sheets were still tangled. Her purse was on the chair in the right corner—just where she'd left it.

The windows appeared to be closed and still locked.

She crept forward. Her body was tight with tension and fear. They'd searched the perimeter for the prowler, but maybe they hadn't found the intruder because he hadn't been outside. He'd been *inside*. The ranch house had been empty. It would have been the perfect time for the guy to sneak in.

No, I must be wrong. I left the lights off.

She bent and searched under the bed. Nothing was there. The closet was empty. She turned toward the bathroom. The door leading to the bathroom was shut, too. Ava tried to remember...

Did I leave it open or closed? She inched forward.

Open?

Another step.

Or closed?

Do not go back to her. Do not. The chant echoed in Mark's head, but his body wanted to turn around and go after Ava. She'd just looked so hurt.

And he'd never wanted to hurt Ava. He wanted to protect her. To keep her safe, always.

Why did he screw up so much when she was around?

Snarling, he turned and marched toward his bathroom. The door was partially shut, and he shoved it open. He flipped on the light—

The glass mirror was shattered. And letters were carved into the wall next to the broken mirror—rough letters that looked as if they'd been made with a shard of that broken glass.

Stay away from her.

"Ava!" He roared her name even as he whirled around and ran from the bathroom. The creep hadn't been outside. He'd been in the house. He'd drawn them out, maybe even set off the alarm deliberately so that he could get access to the home. *"Ava!"* Mark was in the den now and running fast. His heart thundered in his chest. He had to get to Ava, to see her. Had to—

She ran out of her room. "Mark?" Fear flashed on her face.

"He was here," he snarled as he grabbed her shoulders. "Someone was in my home."

She shivered before him. "I...I know." She pointed toward her door. "My light was off. I think he was in my room."

The sick joker might still be in there. Mark pushed her behind his back and ran to her room. The covers were tousled, and he had a flash of Ava in that bed, with him.

So close...

Until that jerk had come and sounded the alarm.

Her bathroom door was shut. Was the guy in there? Waiting for her?

"Be careful," Ava whispered. "I was just about to go in there..."

Forget careful. If someone was waiting in her bathroom, Mark would tear the guy apart. Mark kicked open the door. It slammed back into the nearby wall.

He saw the broken shards of the mirror on the floor. Just like in his bathroom. Words had been left behind for Ava, too. Only these words...

Don't trust him.

"We need to search the whole house," he said, voice flat and hard. "The video cameras were running, so we must have caught the bastard." He turned to find Ava behind him. Her gaze wasn't on Mark, though. It was on the message the intruder had been left behind.

The guy was trying to play games with them, but he was about to realize... Mark was an enemy he didn't want.

No one threatens Ava on my watch.

No one.

THE HOUSE WAS searched from top to bottom. Every closet. Every corner. There was no other sign of the intruder.

Ava's hands were shaking as she watched Mark pull up the video feed from his surveillance cameras. This was the first time the stalker had actually left any kind of message for her.

Don't trust him.

Did the stalker really think she was going to listen to him? She trusted Mark completely. He'd protected her on the worst night of her life. She'd never turn away from him.

"There he is," Mark muttered.

She leaned over his shoulder and...sure enough, she saw a man slipping out of the house.

The guy on the video feed was wearing a black ski mask. And as soon as she saw that ski mask, Ava lost her breath. For a moment in time, she wasn't standing there with Mark, looking at a computer screen. She was back at her old home, hearing the thunder of a gunshot and rushing toward her house. Her father was standing in front of the window.

Run.

And a man wearing a black ski mask was lifting a gun.

"Ava! Ava!"

She blinked. Mark was in front of her, breath heaving. His arms were around her and he was holding her tightly. *Get your control. Don't break in front of him.* Not in front of Mark. He was one of the few who didn't think she was already broken beyond repair. "He... followed me from Houston." She thought of that drive. The darkness. The stretching interstate.

All that time, she thought she'd been leaving him behind, but he'd been with her every step of the way. Had he watched while she'd packed up? Had he been there? Every moment?

Now she'd brought him to Mark's door. No, into Mark's house. "I'm sorry," she whispered, and she pulled away from him. Ava started walking toward the front of the house. Her steps were slow but certain.

"Ava!"

She didn't look back. She'd never wanted to bring danger to Mark, but now she'd put him right in the center of this thing—whatever it was.

But that black ski mask...that wasn't just a coincidence, was it? Was the guy trying to tell her something? *Was he one of the men who killed my parents?* Because those two men had been wearing black ski masks that night.

She reached for the front door. Mark caught her hand and pulled her back against him. Ava tried to break free of him, but he just held her tighter.

"What are you doing?" Mark demanded as she turned in his arms.

"Leaving you."

He flinched.

"I thought that was obvious."

"Why?" He seemed to grit out that one word.

"I'm not going to have you threatened because of me! I won't do that to you!" She owed him more than she could ever repay. Danger wasn't what he deserved.

"He left me a message, too."

Her breath caught.

"The fool told me to stay away from you."

He'd been intimately close to her before the stalker had come calling on them.

Mark's blue eyes glittered down at her. "That's not going to happen. The last thing I'm planning to do is leave you on your own. He wants you to run away. He's trying to put a wedge between us so that you'll be out there, vulnerable, and he can close in on you."

Ava winced. "But what about you?" She hadn't considered the risk to him when she'd driven to his ranch, seeking shelter for the night.

"I can handle anything this guy wants to throw at me." He said the words with such grim certainty. She wanted to believe him.

But, once upon a time, she'd thought another man

could handle any threat that came his way. Then her father had died. He'd died protecting her, and in that moment, she'd vowed—*no one else will ever suffer for me*.

"I want to leave," she told Mark softly.

He shook his head. "No way, baby."

It was the first time he'd ever used any kind of endearment with her. He probably didn't even realize he'd done it. The word didn't mean anything to him, but it had her body warming.

"Yes," she said as she gave a faint nod. "I'm not going to let him hurt you. I'll call the cops. I'll get my brothers involved." Because this situation couldn't be hidden from them, not any longer. They would go into their extreme mode—she had no doubt of that—but she needed to tell them. A strange man had followed her, broken into Mark's place—*he's just getting worse. More dangerous.*

A faint beeping sounded then, coming from Mark's study. His computer. He didn't let Ava go. His fingers curled around her wrist, and he pretty much pulled her back to the study. She stared at the screen there and saw the black SUV that was pulling up to the ranch's gate.

"You don't have to tell them," he said as her brother Davis's tense features came into view. "I think they already know."

"WHAT IS MY SISTER doing at your house—" Davis stalked into the den and headed straight for Mark "—in the middle of the night?"

Mark stood his ground. Ava thought about running for the door—leaving them both.

Instead, she cleared her throat. "It's actually getting

pretty close to dawn now." Davis's green gaze cut to her. She shrugged. "So that's more like morning, not the middle of the night."

He growled. Davis did that. He growled a lot. Once he'd had a much better sense of humor. Then he'd gone off and become a SEAL. Their parents had died—and Davis had locked down his emotions. Hard. Now there was pretty much just one setting for her brother...*ice*.

"How did you know I was here?" she asked him.

"I didn't, not until I saw your car outside." He huffed out a breath. "I was coming by because we're helping to monitor Mark's security system, and when I saw there was some trouble out here earlier, I figured I'd better check it out."

His words just weren't ringing true to her, and Davis hadn't looked her in the eyes while he'd been talking. When Davis lied to her, he never looked her in the eyes.

You're fine, Ava. No one thinks you were involved in what happened to our parents.

He'd been looking right over her shoulder the first time he'd fed her that line of bull. She'd wondered then...had her own brother thought she was involved? Or had he just already heard the rumors that folks were spreading around town?

"Are you sleeping with my sister?"

Now *that* had her eyes flying toward Davis. Her brother was big—as big as Mark. They both had the same broad shoulders and golden skin. But Davis's hair was dark, longer, and his features were rougher than Mark's.

Instead of answering Davis, Mark glared at him. His hands were fisted.

Ava leapt between the two men because it sure

looked as if they were about to come to blows. "Stop it!" Ava ordered. She turned her own glare on Davis. "Mark is my friend, okay? One of the few who stood by me over the years." There had been plenty who turned their backs on her. Folks who actually bought into the story that she'd either planned—or helped to commit— the murder of her parents. "So back off!"

Davis narrowed his eyes, eyes that were a darker green than her own. "What happened here tonight?"

She hesitated.

"Tell him, Ava," Mark urged her gruffly. "Your brothers will track down that maniac."

Exhaling heavily, she nodded. "Someone...someone has been stalking me."

Shock shot across Davis's face. *"What?"*

And she told him everything. From the pictures that had been moved to the cops who hadn't believed her. She told him about how she'd packed up her bags and driven fast to Mark's house...because—

"Why him?" Davis demanded. "Why did you tell him and not us?" He sounded hurt, and that was certainly the last thing she'd wanted.

"I had no actual proof that anyone was doing these things, not until tonight." She pushed back her hair, suddenly feeling very, very weary. The adrenaline high was sure starting to wane. "Then he left those messages here for us."

"What messages?"

"In my bathroom," Ava confessed.

"And mine," Mark added.

Davis's gaze assessed her. "You were sleeping in the guest room."

She nodded. Davis took off, heading down the hallway. In minutes he was back. His eyes immediately locked on Mark. "Did you get the same message?" he asked. "One telling you not to trust my sister?"

Ava glanced over at him. Mark shook his head. "No. Mine was different."

Davis vanished. She figured he'd gone to read the message for himself.

"What did it say?" Her voice was quiet.

His expression unreadable, Mark murmured, "He told me to stay away from you." His eyes glittered down at her. "That isn't happening."

Footsteps pounded—Davis was coming back. Fury was etched onto his face. "Based on what you've said, the stalker's events are seriously escalating! I've seen twisted stuff like this before. Too many times, and it doesn't end well. A man gets fixated on a woman…" His gaze snapped to Mark. "And he can't let her go."

Beside her, Mark tensed.

Then Davis was glancing back at Ava. "You're lucky that you weren't in that room when the guy broke in. Maybe he wouldn't have used that glass just to carve a message on a wall. He might have tried carving into you."

She held her ground. "You think I don't know that?"

Mark swore. "Stop it, Davis. You don't need to scare her."

Right. She was already scared plenty, with Davis adding to her terror.

But Davis fired back, "Maybe she needs to be scared. These incidents have been going on for weeks, and she didn't tell us. She's lucky she isn't already dead."

Ava flinched.

Mark surged toward her brother. "Don't." His voice was low and lethal. "Don't you tell her—"

"Ava is my sister. What is she to you?"

Mark's turbulent stare jumped to her. She thought of the kiss they'd shared in the guest room. Of how very close they'd come to sharing something else, too.

"Ava is—" Mark began.

"He's my friend," Ava said, her words clear and strong. She didn't know what else he might prove to be to her, but on that point, Ava was certain.

Davis opened his mouth to say something else, probably to launch some kind of attack at Mark, but she wasn't in the mood for that. "He was wearing a ski mask."

Davis's brow furrowed.

"A black one." She inclined her head toward the study area. "One of the video cameras caught sight of the guy leaving, so now we know—"

"He's big, probably about six foot one, maybe six foot two," Mark said. "Fit. And far too familiar with my home."

Because he'd just walked right in the door.

"We should get the cops out here," Davis immediately said. "Get them to run a fingerprint check and use their crime-scene team."

Mark's shoulders tensed. "He was wearing gloves in the video, so I don't think the guy left any prints behind. And after our last experience with the cops, I wasn't exactly chomping at the bit to get them here again."

Our last experience. She knew just what he was talking about. For years, the McGuires had been friends with Austin police detective Shayne Townsend. Most of the cops had seemed to give up hope of ever finding the men who'd killed their parents, but Shayne had kept working the case.

Or so they'd all believed.

But when Brodie and his girlfriend had come under attack, they'd all learned the truth about Shayne. The police detective had accidentally killed an unarmed teen years ago, and he'd been covering up the crime ever since. He'd been blackmailed into breaking the law.

And maybe even blackmailed into covering up the identity of the men who'd killed her parents?

That was sure what some of her brothers suspected.

"You never know who you can trust," Davis murmured, his head cocked as he studied Mark. "And who you can't."

There was something in his voice that put Ava on edge.

"We're calling the cops," Davis said. "And I'll want to talk with your men."

Ava shivered a moment, thinking about how close that unknown man had been to her.

Mark pulled out his phone. Spoke quietly.

Davis closed in on her. "Don't trust him."

"Right, I saw the message on the wall. I got it—"

"This message is coming from *me*." His gaze slanted quickly toward Mark, then back to her. "I don't know what you think is happening between you two, but there are things going on you don't know about."

Her back teeth clenched at that. She didn't know about those things only because her brothers liked their secrets. "He's your friend, too."

"I don't know what he is, not right now."

The whole situation was insane. "He saved me that

night." She'd never forget her first sight of him. Terror had filled her, and then—Mark had been there.

Davis exhaled on a rough sigh. "Right before Shayne Townsend died I asked him who killed our parents."

Her heart stopped before pounding again in a double-time rhythm. "What did he say?"

Mark was off the phone. And he'd—he'd closed in on them. "Yeah," Mark said, voice roughening, "what did he say, and why didn't you tell us before now?"

A muscle flexed along the line of Davis's jaw. "I didn't tell you because I know how Ava feels about her *friend* Mark."

She hated the stress he'd just put on that word. "You're friends, too—"

"Montgomery."

"What?" Ava exclaimed. "I don't understand—"

"The last word he said was…Montgomery." Davis turned his attention on a still-as-stone Mark. "So I have to wonder…why did Shayne use his last breath to name *your* family? Unless…the Montgomerys are responsible for the murder of our parents."

She hadn't thought the situation around her could get any worse. But it just had—so very much worse. Because as she stared at Mark, Ava could have sworn that she saw guilt creep across his face.

Chapter Three

"Ava, let me explain," Mark said as he followed her out to her car.

The cops had come out to the ranch. Uniforms who'd questioned them all and who'd collected pretty much zero evidence. Mark wasn't exactly holding his breath when it came to those guys breaking the case wide open. They were still nosing around the place, but Ava was fleeing.

At his words, Ava didn't slow down. Instead, she seemed to speed up as she hurried toward her vehicle. He reached out to stop her.

Davis caught his arm. "I don't think that's a good idea."

Most folks in Austin were afraid of the McGuire brothers. Their reputation preceded them just about everywhere they went. Grant, the eldest brother, was a former army ranger. Davis and his twin, Brodie, were both former SEALs. Mackenzie "Mac" McGuire had been part of Delta Force, and Sullivan, the youngest of the brothers, was an ex-marine. Yeah, most folks hesitated before trying to tangle with those guys.

Mark wasn't most folks. And he'd never taken any crap from the McGuires. "The game has changed," he said, his low voice carrying only to Davis's ears. "I'm not just going to sit back anymore. I thought she was safe. Happy. But she's not. She still wakes up screaming at night. And now some new jerk is out there terrorizing her." He shook his head. "That's not going to happen. She's not going to spend her days and nights afraid. I won't *let* that happen to her." He'd do everything within his power to protect her.

He heard Ava's car door opening. He forced his back teeth to unclench as he said, "Why didn't you come to me about this Shayne Townsend mess weeks ago? I wasn't involved in the murder of your parents! I had plenty of people here at the ranch who saw me right before Ava came galloping up!" The idea that he was involved was ridiculous. He was—

"I know you have an alibi. I already checked that."

Davis had been investigating him?

"It was your father who didn't have an alibi. No one could account for him an hour before the crime or an hour after."

Mark felt shock rip through him. "He was my... *stepfather.*" Like that distinction mattered. Technically, Gregory Montgomery had adopted him. Of course, most folks didn't know that Mark had hated the bastard with every bit of his soul.

"He committed suicide two months after my parents died," Davis said.

Mark glanced over at Ava. She was in her car, appearing for all intents and purposes as if she was about to drive away and leave him.

"Sometimes guilt can drive a man to take his own life."

Davis seriously thinks that Gregory murdered the McGuires!

And…and Mark couldn't say that he hadn't. Because he knew just how twisted Gregory could be.

Ava cranked up her car.

Mark jerked away from Davis. "Ava, wait!" He lunged toward the car. Her window was rolled down, and his fingers pushed through the opening and locked onto the steering wheel. "Wait," he said again, his voice softer.

She didn't look at him.

"I didn't hurt them, Ava."

She nodded. Blinked several times. Oh, no, was she *crying*? He couldn't stand it when Ava cried.

"I would *never* do anything to hurt you."

Again, she gave the faintest of nods.

Davis was a few feet away, watching them far too closely.

"Where are you going?" Mark asked her. "You said you were starting a new job in Austin soon. You can't just stay in some motel." Not with that creep out there watching her. "Stay here. You'll be safe."

Her head turned then, and she finally stared into his eyes. He didn't see any rage there. No accusation. Just the same trust that he always saw when she looked at him. "I don't want to bring any danger to you. He was in your house. Whoever this guy is…I don't want him hurting you."

And I'd be destroyed if he hurt you, Ava. Can't you see that?

"I'm going back to the ranch with Davis."

"You hate staying there." He knew Ava hadn't stepped foot inside the main house, not since that night.

She shrugged. "There's a guest cottage I can use."

"You can stay here." She'd been asking to stay hours before, and now she was running away.

But then Davis stepped forward. "We have better security at our place. He already got in here once. He won't reach her there."

Because the McGuire ranch had basically been transformed into a fortress after those murders. The brothers had wanted to make sure their home was always protected.

Even if that protection had come too late.

"I'm sorry I involved you," Ava said. Her hands were curled around the steering wheel.

He leaned forward a bit more and caught her chin between his thumb and forefinger. "This isn't over, Ava."

"Mark, I—"

He kissed her. A fast, hard kiss, right on her lips. And yes, he knew Davis was watching. So what? It was time all the McGuires realized that Mark would be taking what he wanted.

And what he wanted most was Ava.

He pulled back and held her surprised stare. "I'll be seeing you very soon." She wasn't getting away from him. Not this time.

THE COPS WERE USELESS.

He watched as they scurried around the Montgomery ranch. Were they seriously looking for clues? There weren't any to find. He was too good. He hadn't left any evidence behind, nothing that could be traced to him.

This isn't my first ball game.

And Davis McGuire was there, too. Stalking around, questioning everyone.

Some of the idiots there actually stuttered when they talked to Davis. Like he was some kind of big deal. He wasn't. None of the McGuire brothers were.

The only McGuire who mattered…that was Ava.

She'd left Mark. Good. She'd taken his warning. He'd already known that she was planning to move to Austin. He'd learned that during one of his trips to her place. He liked to keep tabs on Ava. To find out just what was happening in her life.

He was glad that she'd come back home. *Back to me.* He'd grown tired of waiting for her, so he'd started trying to…scare her a bit. Nothing too bad, of course. Just little nudges to make sure Ava realized Houston wasn't the place for her.

She was back now. She'd left Mark.

So it was finally time for him to move in…

I've been waiting, Ava. So patiently. Now you will be mine.

AVA HATED HER family home. It was beautiful, a sprawling ranch with a bluff and a lake, surrounded by old-growth trees. Her father had once said it was a slice of heaven. He'd told her that when her great-grandfather had emigrated from Ireland nearly one hundred years before, he'd taken one look at the land and fallen in love with the place.

Ava didn't think the ranch was heaven. To her, it was much closer to hell.

She parked her car near the small guest house and very much *not* near the main home. When she got out of the vehicle, she wasn't surprised to see Brodie already heading toward her. Brodie and Davis—identical twins who were both way too keen on the overprotective vibe. One look at Brodie's tense face and she knew that Davis had already spilled about the events of the previous night.

She thought he'd lecture her. Instead he pulled her into his arms, nearly crushing her in a giant bear hug. "It's about time you came home."

The words hurt. She knew he didn't mean to hurt her. Brodie loved her. She knew that. But when Brodie looked at the ranch, she knew he saw hope for the future. He and Jennifer were getting married and planning a family. Ava had no doubt the two of them would be deliriously happy there.

When she looked at the ranch, she saw her father telling her to run. She saw blood and death.

"It's…temporary," she told Brodie as she pulled back. "I'll start looking for a new place in the city as soon as—"

"He was wearing a black ski mask."

Right. He'd definitely already gotten the update from Davis. She bet that every one of her brothers had—and, knowing them, they'd be checking in with calls or visits ASAP.

"Give us a few days to figure out what is going on, okay? Then we can get you settled in any place you want to go."

Any place…

For some reason, she thought of Mark.

He'd kissed her before she left. Had Davis told Brodie that bit, too? Wasn't a woman supposed to have some secrets?

Brodie eased back and headed toward her trunk. "Let's get you settled."

Her gaze slid toward the stables. Lady was in there. She used to love riding Lady. Riding fast and hard and feeling the wind whip through her hair.

"Ava?"

"You all should have told me about what Shayne said." She glanced over at him. "I could have told you it was bull. Mark wasn't involved."

Brodie's gaze became guarded. "Can you say the same thing about his old man?"

Honestly, she barely remembered him. The man hadn't come over to their place very much, and he certainly hadn't socialized often in the community. Gregory Montgomery had kept to himself, and there had been some rumors that he drank…heavily.

But since Ava had been the topic of plenty of rumors that called her a murderer, she hadn't exactly believed those tales about Gregory.

"They were engaged once," Brodie said. "Mom and Gregory Montgomery."

"What?" She sure hadn't seen that little tidbit coming.

"But then she met dad, and everything changed for her. She broke off the engagement to Gregory, she eloped with Dad…and, well, you know how the rest of that story went."

The rest of the story ended with their parents *dying*.

"That's why Mr. Montgomery didn't come over much. Word is that he and our dad used to be good friends, but there are some things that can change a man."

She looked at the lake. The water glistened. She should stare at it and think it was beautiful. Instead, a shiver slid over her as she gazed at the water.

"We'll find the man doing this to you," Brodie promised her. "No one messes with my family."

No, those who'd tried—well, they'd found a lethal response waiting from Brodie in the past. "Is Jennifer doing better?" Ava asked. Because his girlfriend—*fiancée, now*—Jennifer had been attacked, and her attacker had died. *Lethal response.*

He smiled. His dimples flashed. "She's great. She'll be back in town tonight, and she can't wait to see you."

Jennifer was an interesting woman. On the surface, Ava had thought the woman was a sophisticated, high-society type. Then she'd learned the truth—Jennifer was a tough ex-spy who'd worked to bring down some of the most vicious criminals in the world.

"What you see…" Ava murmured…*is so far from what you actually get.*

She headed around the car and grabbed one of her bags.

Ava HEADED INTO the city during the middle of the day. She stopped by the art museum and checked in. She spent a little time talking with her new supervisor, Kristin Lang. Ava wasn't scheduled to start for a few days, but she still wanted to get the lay of the land. After her chat with Kristin, she spent some time just walking around the place and admiring the art.

When she'd first started college, art had been her passion. On too many occasions it was the only way that she could get through so many of those long nights. She hadn't wanted to talk to a therapist or one of the counselors at the college. After a couple of group sessions, she'd withdrawn from the group. Baring her soul to them had just made her feel even more broken. Instead she'd painted.

Ava had painted canvases full of darkness and rage. So much red—for the blood and the rage. Rage that would course through her so strongly. She'd been furious at the men who killed her parents and furious with herself because she should have been able to help them, but she hadn't. She'd done nothing but run.

Some of her art teachers had seen her working at the studio. They'd wanted her to show her work.

But she couldn't. It was too raw. Too personal. Too... much of her soul.

So when she'd gone to graduate school, she'd focused on art history. She'd lucked out by getting this job. She'd thought about applying for a position far away, maybe taking a job up north or in the east—

"Ava?"

She turned at the call and found herself staring into a pair of warm golden eyes.

Her gaze swept over him. "Alan?"

"I thought that was you!" He smiled at her, flashing perfectly even white teeth. Then he opened his arms and pulled her into a big hug. "It's been so long!"

Years.

She pulled back. He'd changed from the boy she'd known so long ago. His features were sharper. His blond hair was stylishly pushed back from his forehead. His clothes—perfectly cut. Alan Channing had always been gifted with plenty of money and pull.

And once, he'd almost had her. At sixteen, she'd thought she loved him. She'd learned—just in time— that Alan wasn't the boy she'd thought.

The night my parents died, I was supposed to be with him.

"I heard that you were going to be working here." His grin grew even broader. "I was just appointed to the art museum's board, so we'll probably be seeing a lot of each other."

Her gut clenched at that news, but Ava forced a polite

smile. "Oh, really? That's just—" She broke off, unable to think of a polite lie because *That's just terrible* wanted to spill from her lips.

"I'm not the same, Ava." Alan's voice deepened as his smile slipped. "I'm not the same jerk I was back then."

She lifted her brows. "I don't remember calling you a jerk." Hmm...or had she?

Alan laughed. "Not now, but back then you did. Jerk and plenty of other things—and you were right. I didn't realize what a total screw-up I was." His face sobered. "Then...then your parents died. I saw how wrecked you were. Things changed for a lot of people back then."

How wrecked she'd been? And she remembered that Alan had tried to talk to her—at the funeral, at school in the weeks that followed. But she hadn't been able to talk with anyone back then. She'd been walking around in a fog, barely able to get through the days.

By the time she'd come out of her grief, the whispers had started.

Did she kill them? Was she in on it?

And she'd just wanted to run.

Maybe...maybe it was time she stopped running.

Isn't that why I took this job in Austin? Instead of heading up north? Because, deep down, she'd known that she couldn't run forever.

Her spine straightened as she stared at him. "I guess we both changed."

"We have." Alan's head inclined toward her. "Hey, how about we go out and grab some lunch? We can catch up, and perhaps I can start making up for being such a fool all those years ago."

Ava shook her head. "Sorry, but I have to go back and meet my brothers."

He took a step back. "Right. The brothers." Alan gave a little shudder. "You know, they used to terrify me. I was almost too afraid to ask you out."

She laughed at that. "Oh, Alan...they still terrify people." Then she eased past him.

"I'll be seeing you, Ava," he murmured, and his hand lightly caressed her arm.

For an instant, she stilled as a shiver slid over her. It wasn't the same kind of sensual shiver she got when Mark touched her. This was something else. Something...that was almost like a warning.

Her steps quickened as she hurried away from Alan.

Ava headed for the front of the museum. Her heels clicked over the marble floor and—

Mark was there. Striding through the entrance and heading right for her.

She stopped. Just froze for a second. His gaze swept around the museum, and then his eyes locked on her. It was rather like watching a hunter lock in on his prey. His saw her, his face tightened and then he began to stride right toward her.

Her breath quickened as she shook out of her stupor and hurried toward him, too. When they drew closer, she asked, "What are you doing here?"

His lips tightened.

"Did you follow me?" Her voice rose on that one. No, surely he hadn't—

"Some nut broke into my house and threatened you last night." He yanked a hand through his hair. "So, yes, that made me worry about you a bit. When I found out you were in town—"

"*How* did you find that out?"

"Brodie told me."

Well, wonderful, they were all tracking her now. That was what she'd feared. *Hello, hyperprotective mode.*

"Since he told me where you were, I guess that means he doesn't think I'm involved in what happened to your parents."

"None of them think *you* were involved." She didn't want to talk about his father, not then. "And I don't need you following me."

His gaze tracked over her shoulder. "Is that the little jerk you used to date? The one who stood you up for homecoming?" Anger roughened his voice.

She nearly rolled her eyes. She did quicken her step and head right for the gleaming glass doors that would take her out of the museum. "Yes, that's Alan Channing. And no, he didn't stand me up. I broke up with him right before homecoming." They were outside now, and the heat of the city blasted her. Memories were stirring in her mind, and she found herself blurting, "I heard him bragging about having sex with me to some of his football buddies. He was saying that he'd spend five minutes at the dance with me, then have me naked in the motel room ten minutes later." At the time, those words had shattered her.

Then she'd learned there were much, much worse things in life than just the words of some ex-boyfriend.

"He said *what*?" Mark demanded. Fury was stamped on his face. Then he spun on his heel and started charging right back up to the museum.

"Whoa! Wait!" She grabbed him as understanding hit her. He'd been going back in there to find Alan. And do what? "That was a long time ago."

"There's no expiration date on a whooping."

Her jaw dropped. "You are not serious!"

"If he said that about you—" his eyes were a blue fire "—then yes, I'm dead serious."

And she'd thought her brothers were bad. "He was a teenager. He said something stupid and I dumped him. End of story." She'd handled it on her own. "I don't need you fighting this battle for me." There was no battle there *to* fight.

"But he...hurt you."

For some reason, those words made her heart ache. "Do you know who I haven't thought about? Not once in all of these years?"

The door to the museum opened. Alan appeared.

Really bad timing, Alan.

"Him," she told Mark as she slid closer to him. Both of her hands were on Mark's shoulders now because she was more than a little worried he might break away and drive his fist into Alan's perfect smile. "Because he didn't matter after that night."

She could feel the tension in Mark's body.

"So let it go," she told him. "I sure have."

His gaze dropped to her lips. Then he leaned forward. Kissed her—not hard and deep. But softly. Carefully. "I just don't want," he whispered against her mouth, "anyone hurting you."

Warmth spread through her. Mark had to feel some of the same emotions that she did. And he was kissing her—again! Making her feel like she mattered to him. More than anything.

"Well..." That was Alan's slightly nasal voice. "I thought you were meeting your brothers, Ava."

"You should really let me throw at least one punch at him," Mark murmured.

"No," she snapped back at him. Then she looked at Alan. "You know Mark Montgomery, don't you?"

Alan nodded once, stiffly. "I believe you're on the board here, too, aren't you, Montgomery? When I signed on, they were telling me the names of a few others that I'd be working with."

"Yeah, I'm on the board." Mark's voice was flat.

Wait, both of them? And suddenly she was wondering just *why* she'd been offered the plum job at the art museum.

"I didn't realize the two of you were...involved," Alan said. He smiled at her, but it certainly wasn't the big grin he'd worn before. Far more forced and coldly polite.

"It's new," Mark said blandly. "She came back to town and—boom. I wasn't about to let her go again."

Alan's gaze slid to Ava. Softened. "I understand." He nodded to them. "If you'll excuse me, I have a meeting that's waiting."

A meeting that hadn't been waiting before when he'd asked her out to lunch?

He hurried down the stairs. She kept a close eye on Mark, making sure he wasn't going to go all macho on her and try to take a swing at the guy. "I think he's a bit afraid of you." Alan had sure fled fast enough. "Why would he be afraid?" she asked. Her brothers, she got. But Mark?

He shrugged. His fingers caught hers. He lifted her hand to his mouth and pressed a quick kiss to the back of her knuckles. "Don't know. Don't care."

"I...I have to go meet my brothers." They'd planned

a family dinner for her. And she wanted to check in and see if they'd discovered anything else about her stalker.

I didn't see anyone suspicious today or have the weird feeling that I was being watched. She'd felt that way a few times, back in Houston. Today had been different.

"Are you staying at the guest house?"

She nodded. "You know I can't stand the thought of sleeping in the main house." Honestly, being in that guest cottage was too close for her comfort.

"Then I guess I'll be seeing you soon." His fingers slowly released hers. But he didn't back away.

Neither did she, because she had to know. "Why?"

His brows lifted.

"You've been keeping me at a distance for so long." She wasn't going to waste time trying to hint around at this thing between them. "And now you're kissing me in public? Touching me?" *Almost having sex with me in your guest room.* "Why now?"

But he didn't speak. He just stood there.

Ava shook her head. "What is it that you want from me?"

"Everything."

MARK MONTGOMERY WAS a problem. The fool wasn't backing away from Ava. He was following her, trying to get closer to her, to kiss her.

And Ava—he'd warned her about Mark. Why couldn't she see him for the jerk that he was? Mark wasn't some hero to save the day.

He was a killer. Cold-blooded. Evil to the core. He didn't deserve Ava.

He didn't deserve any happiness.

It was time to make Mark pay for the things he'd done. And when Mark fell, when Mark lost all that he had, then Ava would see the man for the liar and betrayer that he really was.

He's not the one for you, Ava. I am.

When would she ever learn the truth? Just how much more would he have to do before she appreciated him?

Cars whizzed past him on the street. Ava pulled away from Mark. She hurried down the steps. Mark watched her, his gaze far too intent on her fleeing figure.

She's not for you.

Mark would learn that lesson soon enough.

Chapter Four

They had dinner at the guest cottage. It was sweet, really, the way Davis prepared all of the food up at the ranch and then brought it over to her. Davis was actually an amazing chef, and whenever she ate one of his meals, Ava knew she was tasting a bit of paradise.

Grant came with his wife, Scarlett. As soon as she'd entered the cottage, Scarlett had pulled Ava close and whispered, "Are you okay?"

Scarlett had her own violent and far-too-scary past, so if any woman could understand Ava's pain, it was her. Ava had nodded even as she blinked away the ridiculous tears that had wanted to sting her eyes.

Brodie and Jennifer had come over for dinner, too. They'd talked, laughed and tried to keep Ava distracted. Oh, she'd recognized the technique for exactly what it was.

But when the meal came to an end, she got down to business. "Did you find out anything about the man who broke into Mark's house?"

Davis slanted a quick glance toward Grant, then shook his head. "No, the guy's pretty good. Made it on to the property without leaving any signs of a break-in.

He slipped inside during the confusion caused by that alarm sounding at the stables—"

"Betting he set that off deliberately," Brodie interrupted with a quick nod.

"Why?" Jennifer asked. "He made it that far without sounding the alarm, so why do it then."

"So that there *would* be plenty of confusion," Brodie said flatly as his gaze slid to Jennifer.

Brodie and Davis looked so much alike. The only difference? Brodie's face softened when he glanced at Jennifer.

And he glanced at her plenty. Jennifer's dark hair had been pulled back into a loose knot at the base of her head. Her dark eyes gleamed when she looked at Brodie. They...warmed.

It was obvious those two loved each other deeply. Just as much as Grant and Scarlett loved each other. Ava couldn't help but wonder...what would it be like to have a man love her that way? So completely?

"I think he did it to draw Mark away, too," Davis added. "No one was in the house but the two of them. With Mark gone, the guy had free access to Ava."

That sounded bad. Very bad. "He hasn't tried to hurt me before."

"He's escalating," Grant said flatly. "That's why you should have told us about this joker before. I mean, we're family and—"

"You had enough to deal with." That was a serious understatement. "And at first, I started to wonder if the cops were right. Maybe I was imagining things." Hadn't she worried in those first desperate days that she might be going crazy with the grief and the guilt that wouldn't end?

"Ava…" Sympathy flashed in Davis's eyes—sympathy and pity.

They weren't the same thing. Not at all. And she hated the pity.

Then Davis's phone rang. No, it didn't ring so much as it gave off a chiming alarm. He pulled out the phone and frowned at the screen. "I've got the gate's security system linked in here," he said as he lifted the phone. "It looks like we've got company out there." He tapped the display. "It's Mark."

Her body tensed. She looked up quickly—and found Scarlett's gaze on her. There was no pity in Scarlett's face, just plenty of speculation.

"What is he doing here now?" Brodie muttered.

"Can't a friend pay a visit?" Ava shot back as she jumped to her feet. If Davis wasn't going to key in the pass code to let Mark inside the ranch, then she'd go bring him in herself. "Let him in, Davis."

Davis tapped in a code on his phone.

Ava exhaled and hurried for the door. "Maybe he's found out something about the break-in."

"Yeah," Brodie drawled from behind her, "and he just had to come over and tell us in person instead of, you know, picking up the phone."

She stepped outside. She could see the lights from Mark's car coming up the curving drive. Mark wasn't heading for the main ranch house. He was coming to the little guest house—to her. Her family had filed out behind her.

"Do you know what you're doing with him?" Davis asked her softly. "Ava…there's more to him than you know."

She turned to stare at him. They were on the narrow

porch, and the front door light felt as though it was spearing down on her, bright, stark. "There's more to me than he knows, too." *More than you all know.*

She wasn't going to hide from the past any longer. It was time to face the nightmares. "I want in on the hunt."

"Ava, you don't need that pain," Grant said instantly.

"I've already got plenty of pain. Staying in the dark doesn't stop it."

Davis shook his head.

Brodie swore.

"You've tried to shut me out for years." Did they have any idea how much that had hurt? "You hunted for the killers, and you kept me in the dark."

"We were protecting you," Brodie grated out.

"I'm not a child anymore. I don't need you to shield me from the world. I can help. I *will* help."

Mark parked his SUV. He jumped out, then slammed the door behind him.

Ava could feel his stare on her as he approached. There was just something there—a connection that seemed to make her hypersensitive to him.

"I was coming back to Austin," Ava said, her voice low but firm, "even before this creep started messing with me. It's not about me running from him. It's about me…facing my life." A life that was there, in Austin.

"Thanks for letting me in," Mark said as he closed in on them. "I came to see Ava."

"Right," Brodie said, voice tight. "I heard all about how you *saw* her this morning and last night."

Jennifer slapped his shoulder. "Oh, Brodie, stop acting crazy. Ava's an adult, Mark's an adult and you need to chill out."

Mark braced his legs apart as he faced them. "If any

of you think I had something to do with the death of your parents, say it now."

Her brothers didn't say a word.

"The McGuires have been my friends for as long as I can remember. Yeah, Gregory used to get mad because he didn't want me around you all, but…he wasn't me. *And I'm not like him.* If he did anything, *anything at all*, to your parents, if he was involved in any way, I swear to you, I will find out the truth." His breath heaved out. "I protected that SOB while he was alive. I did it for my mother's sake."

A mother who'd passed away when Mark was a teen, right before his eighteenth birthday. Mark had vanished for a time after that and had only come back…right before Ava's parents had been murdered.

She wasn't sure what he'd done in those years, but judging from the way Davis kept talking about Mark, she strongly suspected her brother was aware of his secrets.

"He liked to hurt people." Mark's shoulders rolled back. "Me in particular. And yeah, you probably already know that he hated your father. He blamed the man for taking the one woman who Gregory said was perfect."

Ava couldn't move.

"He loved your mother, or at least, as much as he could love anyone. When my mom came around, he thought she was beautiful. I heard him say once that he had to claim the most beautiful woman around. That it would show the McGuires. I don't even know if he ever loved my mother. He sure didn't love me."

Ava broke from her stupor and hurried toward Mark. He was baring his soul in front of them.

"I stayed until she was gone, and I came back—

because I knew he was bad. I was taking steps to get him in rehab, but he didn't want help. He just wanted to die."

And he had. Ava stopped at Mark's side. But then she realized that wasn't good enough. She wrapped her arms around him and held him close. "I'm sorry," she whispered.

She and her brothers had been caught up in their own pain for so long. What about Mark? What about his pain and his life?

Even heroes needed help.

He was tense against her. "If he was involved, I'll find out."

She pulled back just enough to look up at his face.

Their gazes locked. Tension thickened in the air.

"Um…right…" Jennifer cleared her voice. "I think we should probably pack it in for the night. Brodie, Davis, how about we head up to the main house? Let's give them a chance to…to talk."

"Yes," Scarlett agreed instantly. "Grant, we should leave and head home, too. You're supposed to call your other brothers, remember?"

Because Sullivan and Mac were out working cases, they hadn't been able to join the dinner-slash-grilling-Ava-with-questions event.

Footsteps shuffled forward. Ava glanced over and saw Davis hesitate. He inclined his head toward Mark. "I know what he did to you. I hated it. I saw the scars, man. Not until too late, but I saw them. By then, he was already in the ground."

And Ava remembered touching Mark's back, feeling the raised flesh beneath her fingertips. Scars?

A dark picture formed in her mind, and nausea rolled

in her stomach. If her suspicions were right, then Mark had suffered far more than she'd realized.

"I thought about putting him in the ground myself," Mark admitted starkly. "That's why I left."

Davis glanced at Ava once more. They'd moved away from the light, so it was hard for her to see his expression.

"Ava has nightmares," Mark murmured. "I just... I want to make sure she's okay before I leave."

Jennifer was pulling Brodie toward the main house while Scarlett dragged Grant to their car.

Davis exhaled. "I guess Ava's always safe...when she's with you."

"I'd protect her with my life."

No, that *wasn't* something she wanted to happen. She never wanted him to be put at risk for her. She didn't want *any* of them put at risk for her. She had enough guilt on her soul to last several lifetimes already.

"So would I," Davis said softly. Then he turned and walked away.

That was the problem—they were all willing to risk too much for her. Didn't they get it? She was determined to protect them, too, at all costs. They all mattered to her. Her family. Mark. She'd protect them with her life. Because she would never run while someone she loved died. Never again.

She and Mark stood in silence for a few moments. Ava was waiting for the others to clear out before she spoke. There were some things she just didn't want her brothers to hear.

Like...

"How many secrets do you have?" Ava asked Mark, her voice quiet. The others were far enough away now that she didn't think they would overhear her. "I used to think that, with you, what I saw—"

"Surfaces lie. People lie." His words sounded gruff. "You should be careful who you trust in this world."

"I trust you." *With no hesitation.*

His hand lifted. His knuckles slid over her cheek. "I know."

"Are you trying to tell me that this is wrong? That I shouldn't?" Ava shook her head. "Because if that's the case, you should save your breath."

Then she turned and headed back to the guest house. He didn't follow her. Sighing, she stopped near the door. "Are you coming inside, Mark? Or did you drive all the way over here just so you could hang out in the dark?"

He gave a short bark of laughter, one that surprised her. She didn't think that she'd heard Mark laugh much over the years. And actually, Ava wasn't even sure she could remember the last time she'd laughed herself.

But I want to laugh again. I want to laugh and be happy and fall in love. I want to be just like everyone else. She was tired of feeling like a ghost, just drifting through the days. She wanted more from life.

I want to live and not just go through the motions.

"As tempting as the dark is—" his footsteps padded closer "—I came to see you."

Now that was what she'd hoped to hear. Ava opened the door and slipped through. Mark followed her. And as soon as he stepped inside, the guest house seemed even smaller.

No, she was just far more aware of him. Because they were alone now. No prying eyes. No overprotective brothers.

Time to find out just how much Mark would truly reveal to her.

Ava shut the door behind him. Then she braced her back against the wood and stared up at him. "I don't know how to play games."

He raised a brow as he gazed at her.

"My last boyfriend...that was Alan Channing. You know how that ended."

"Your last—" he began, voice incredulous.

"I've tried dating a few times," she said, cutting through his words. "But nothing clicked for me." Because by then...she'd already been comparing every man she met to Mark. "So I'm not used to all the sweet little lies that lovers are supposed to tell one another. And...I don't want to lie to you, Mark."

His expression hardened.

"So I'm just going to say this...I want you." She could feel her cheeks heat with her confession. "I know things are crazy now." When had they not been for her? "But when I kiss you, I'm not playing some kind of game. I'm kissing you because I need to do it. I ache when you're near."

His eyes squeezed closed. "Ava..."

"Why do you kiss me, Mark? Do you want me, too?"

His eyes opened. Desire was there, burning bright and igniting the blue of his stare. "More than you can even imagine."

Ava wasn't so sure about that. She could imagine a whole lot.

He moved toward her. The hardwood creaked beneath his feet. She tensed as he approached. It was a helpless, instinctive reaction. His hands came up and flattened behind her, effectively caging her between his body and the door.

"I kiss you," he told her, voice rough and rumbling—and making her toes curl a bit, "because I love the way you taste. I love it when you moan for me. When your breath goes ragged…"

Her breath was pretty ragged right then.

"I love the feeling of your mouth against mine. I've been thinking about that mouth of yours…" And his stare was on her lips. Lips that had parted as if she were waiting for his kiss. "Ever since that night two years ago."

"Christmas." Her whisper was husky.

"You were under the mistletoe. You weren't smiling and laughing like everyone else." His head lowered, came closer to hers. "You should have been. Beautiful Ava, you should have been the life of the party."

She hadn't even wanted to be at that party. She'd gone to the Christmas party at McGuire Securities for her brothers. She'd been wishing she could run away from that crowd. But then…

"I touched your hand. You looked up at me, and you smiled. Your first smile that whole night."

Had he been watching her that entire time?

"I kissed you. Even as I did it, I knew it was wrong. That you weren't meant for me."

She didn't want anyone else.

"Then I tasted you." His mouth was so close to hers. She wanted to taste him right then. "And I was lost. I knew I'd never get enough of you."

Her heart was a mad drumbeat in her chest. "But you…you stayed away." For so long. He hadn't tried to touch her again. Hadn't kissed her—

Until I was back at his ranch. In that bedroom.

"I'm not the man you need."

So wrong. "You're the man I want."

Then she stopped waiting for him to kiss her. Ava wrapped her arms around him and pulled Mark close. She kissed him, pressing her lips to his because she loved his taste, too. She loved the way kissing him made her feel. Already her blood was heating. Arousal deepened within her. She'd been waiting a long time for this man...and she was done waiting.

The wood was hard against her back, and he was so strong before her. In his arms, she wasn't afraid. She wasn't thinking about the past. It was just...him. That moment.

"I want to be with you," she whispered against his lips.

He kissed her harder. Deeper. His tongue slid into her mouth and she moaned. Her breasts were aching. She wanted him—wanted him in her.

This wasn't some frantic one-night stand. This was Mark. This was...everything.

His hands moved away from the wood. They locked around her hips, then slid down, curving around her and pulling Ava flush against him. There was no missing the force of desire.

He wants me, too.

"I can't even think clearly when you're close." His words were ragged. So deep. "I want you naked. I want to kiss every inch of your body."

Um, yes, that sounded more than good to her. It was a fabulous, fabulous plan. She'd love to explore his body. Kiss the scars she'd felt on his back. See if she could make him growl with desire. See if she could drive him as wild as he drove her.

"But I want to do things right with you." He pressed a kiss to her throat. Right there, at the base of her neck. The spot that made her quiver. The spot he'd found. "And I'm not going to rush you."

He pulled back.

No!

"You're not rushing me." How was he missing this? She felt like jumping him!

"Your brothers are watching, waiting for me to leave." He shook his head. "When I take you, I'm going to want the whole night. Because when I get you in my bed, I'm not planning to let you leave anytime soon."

She didn't want him leaving then.

"Mark…"

He kissed her again. "I needed you to know," he murmured against her lips, "that you can count on me."

She already had known that.

"My secrets, my past—I won't let them hurt you."

Ava shook her head.

"Lock the door behind me," he said.

He was leaving? "Stay," she said.

She could see the struggle on his face.

"Mark…"

But he reached for the doorknob. "You need your rest, and you also need to think about what's going to happen when we cross this line between us."

The line between friends and lovers. She was ready to race across that line. Full speed ahead!

"There won't be any going back." His words were a warning, and his expression had darkened. "I don't think I can have you once, then watch you walk away."

She wasn't going anyplace.

"I've seen a man's obsession for a woman wreck his world."

He had to be talking about Gregory Montgomery.

"I already think I'm half-obsessed with you. You should…be very careful with me." He opened the door.

She caught his hand. "You're nothing like him."

"I don't have his blood, but I lived in his house for years. There were things that happened there, things I don't talk about much."

"He hurt you." And that knowledge enraged her.

Mark stared down at her.

"I touched the scars on your back."

His shoulders lifted in a small shrug. "When he didn't like the way I worked the ranch, he'd use his belt."

Ava flinched.

"I was thirteen the first time he came after me. And I didn't know what I was supposed to be doing at the ranch. I learned, fast, not ever to make the same mistake twice."

"Mark…" She started to wrap her arms around him, but he stiffened.

"I don't want your pity, Ava."

And wasn't that why she responded so deeply to him? Because he didn't look at her with pity in his beautiful gaze? "I don't pity you," she said clearly. "I just want to hurt Gregory." In that instance, she figured it was a shame the dead couldn't be hurt.

"He never touched my mother. Never let the ranch hands see what he did. I was dependent on him. He'd adopted me, taken us both in. I knew that if we left him, my mother and I would have nothing. Everything, *everything* was his."

Her hands fisted. "You should have told us. My brothers—"

"Like Davis said, he figured out what was happening. It was right before my mom died. When she passed, I didn't care anymore. I left. Rode out fast and hot, and I *wanted* that bastard to die, too."

But Gregory hadn't died, not then. He'd lived for years—and then Mark had come home.

And my parents died just a few days later.

"You are not like him," she said, the words tight. *He was a monster.* Mark wasn't. He was good and strong and—

"Everyone has darkness inside. We can all be pushed too far." His breath heaved out slowly. "Remember that, when you're making your choice. Because I've got more darkness in me than you probably can even guess."

Davis...he'd said something before about Mark and—

"I want you too much. Maybe you should play it safe and tell me to stay away."

She shook her head. Why couldn't he see she wanted him the same way? "I'm not afraid of you." Not of any part of him. Good, bad, darkness, light—whatever, it didn't matter.

"Maybe you should be." He inclined his head. "Lock the door, Ava."

Then he was striding away and heading back to his SUV.

She shut the door.

Locked it.

A few moments later, she heard his vehicle crank. Mark drove away.

Maybe you should be.

THE GATES OF the McGuire ranch shut behind him. Mark paused a moment, his vehicle idling. He was trying to do the right thing with Ava, but every time he got close to her, he just—wanted.

Wanted her naked.

Wanted to see her flush with pleasure.

And—

Her voice, soft and husky, echoed through his mind. *My last boyfriend...that was Alan Channing.*

And that guy was a serious grade-A jerk.

His fingers tightened around the steering wheel.

Keep moving. Drive away. Now.

He shifted gears and drove down that dark road. He hadn't been kidding when he'd told Ava that he worried he was already half-obsessed with her. He thought about her too much. Wanted to protect her at all times. Wanted to destroy anyone who threatened her—

I should let her go. She deserves more.

Because he'd lied to Ava before. Lied to the McGuires. Lied to the police. There were things he'd done that would always darken his soul. Things he never wanted Ava to know about.

Some secrets were better left buried with the dead. They couldn't hurt anyone then. They couldn't destroy a life.

He headed east, traveling back to his ranch. He thought of Ava as she'd last been, standing there with her eyes so big and deep, with her cheeks lightly flushed and her lips slightly swollen from his kiss.

Walking away from her then had been one of the hardest things he'd ever done. He wasn't sure he'd be able to pull away from her next time. He'd warned Ava. Now the choice was hers.

There were no other vehicles on the old dark road. His headlights cut through the night as his SUV ate up the distance to his ranch. He paused at his gate, slowing while he waited to head inside and—

The gunshot blasted. It hit his windshield, the boom like that of a firecracker exploding.

Even as Mark slammed down the gas pedal and the SUV shot forward, more shots were firing, striking the windows and the hood of his SUV in fast succession. Glass rained down on him and a bullet blazed right across his arm.

He needed to make it inside his property. He could get help if he could make it inside—

A bullet hit his front tire. One bullet, then another in fast succession. The SUV swerved as he tried to steady the wheel, but it was too late. The SUV broke through the fence, then barreled into a tree.

AVA PACED AROUND the guest cottage. Tension was knotting her gut. She kept thinking about Mark. About the choices people made in life.

About the choices she'd made.

No more running.

She stared out the window. It was so dark out there. She couldn't even see the stars right then because storm clouds had rolled in. She'd heard the forecast for that night. She knew a powerful storm was supposed to sweep into the area before dawn.

As she gazed at the dark sky, lightning flashed for a moment, a bright streak that stretched like spindly fingers in the night.

Then she heard the crack of thunder. Only...

Her phone beeped. Ava turned around. She took a

few steps and found her phone on the table near the door. When she picked it up, Ava saw that she'd just gotten a text from Mark.

Ava, I need you. Come meet me at my ranch.

Her breath caught and her fingers tightened around the phone. No, there would be no more running away for her. This time, she'd be running *to* someone.

She'd waited long enough. Time to start living.

She hurried from the guest house. Lightning flashed once more.

MARK'S EYES CRACKED OPEN. The pain hit him first, exploding in his head and he realized that he'd slammed into the steering wheel. His air bag hadn't deployed— and the dash was smashed, pretty much caging him in the SUV. Broken glass littered the area around him. He could feel cuts on his arms, and the skin near his right shoulder burned—

Because some SOB took shots at me!

His memory returned in a flash. He'd wrecked and hit his head so hard that he must have lost consciousness for a few moments. He pushed against the mangled steering wheel and dash, trying to twist out, but there was no give there. He was pinned too tightly.

Fumbling, he tried to grab for his phone, but—

It wasn't there. It should have been in the dock near the radio. Who knew where the thing had flown in the crash? The *dock* was gone. The driver's side door was open, swaying drunkenly, freedom so close.

But he couldn't reach it. He was trapped.

And that psycho with the gun could still be out there.

Fumbling, he tried to reach for the glove compartment. He kept a screw driver in that glove box. Not much of a weapon, but far better than nothing. And maybe he could use the screw driver to help pry himself out of that tangled mess. He stretched and his fingers slid over the edge. Almost...almost...

He couldn't reach it.

Blood dripped into his eyes and lightning flashed.

He was a sitting duck. The shooter could come in for him at any moment, and Mark wouldn't even be able to move.

DROPS OF RAIN pelted down on Ava as she hurried to her car. She glanced up at the ranch house. Lights still glowed up there. If she just vanished in the middle of the night, her brothers would worry.

Her phone chimed again.

Ava, don't make me wait long.

Her breath rushed out.

Come alone, sweetheart. I want to make love to you again.

Her drumming heartbeat grew even faster right then, because—she and Mark had never made love. And he'd never called her sweetheart.

Baby. He slipped up and called me baby *once. But not sweetheart.*

She ran toward the ranch house. For an instant, the past and present blurred. It was another night. She'd heard thunder—

I heard thunder a few moments ago.

She was running to the house, looking toward that big picture window…

Ava skidded to a stop. The big picture window was gone. Her brothers had remodeled the ranch house. The window she remembered from her nightmares had been torn down long ago.

The house looked so different now. A new place. There were flowers running around the house, and—

Lightning flashed.

Ava ran toward the door. She pounded her fist against it. *Hurry, hurry.* They weren't answering fast enough. She grabbed the doorknob and twisted, but it was locked. So she pounded again and again and—

"Ava?" Davis had yanked open the door. "What's going on?" He grabbed her wrist and tried to pull her into the house. "Is someone here? Did something happen?"

She jerked away from him. "Mark's in trouble!" She was certain of it. "We have to go help him, *now*!"

Chapter Five

Low, rough laughter reached Mark's ears.

He stopped struggling when he heard that sound.

"She's coming…" the voice rasped. It came from too close by.

His headlights must have been busted out because they weren't throwing off any illumination. The interior of the SUV was a dark hole.

"She thinks that she's coming to you. Ava is racing to see her lover again, but she won't find you." The voice was still low. The jerk was trying to disguise himself.

Mark rammed against that steering wheel once more. Had it shifted just a little bit?

"She won't find you, though. I'll be waiting for Ava."

No, no, that couldn't happen. "You stay away from her!" Mark yelled as he heaved with all of his strength.

"You're the one who should have stayed away." It sounded like the guy was moving. Circling around the SUV? Yes, Mark could just see the guy's outline. He was near the smashed front of the vehicle, raising his arm as lightning flashed. In that instant, Mark saw the gun gripped in the other man's hand. "I warned you, but you just didn't listen, did you?"

Mark surged against that wheel. Yes, *yes*, it had

shifted, just an inch, but an inch was all he needed. He could slide out now. But first he had to get a weapon. He also had to distract the assailant who had Mark locked in his sights.

"Ava isn't yours. She was never meant for you."

Mark forced himself to laugh. "Let me guess. You think Ava belongs to you?" His fingers slid over the passenger seat. He found a chunk of glass that had once been part of the passenger-side window. That chunk would have to do. Not a knife, but he could still do some serious injury with that thing.

Another part of my life that Ava doesn't know about. I learned to kill, maybe too well.

He had more in common with her brothers than Ava realized.

"Ava is mine!" The voice was even lower. Mark had to strain to hear it. His eyes were trying to adjust to the darkness, and he thought the guy was wearing a hood...no, a mask.

Lightning flashed again.

A dark ski mask.

"I've had plans for Ava ever since she was sixteen."

Mark's blood turned to ice in his veins. "You killed her parents."

Laughter. Laughter that he hated. "I'll kill anyone who gets between Ava and me. She came back for me, and now I get to keep her." He was raising that weapon. Mark saw the guy's hand lift—

Mark jumped out the driver's side door. The bullet erupted less than a second later, slamming into the driver's seat. Mark hit the ground hard, and he rolled, twisting and coming up as fast as he could. There were trees all around there, plenty of space for cover, and he leapt for them, his heart racing fast and his legs pumping furiously.

Another shot sounded, and a chunk of bark flew off the tree near his head. *Missed me! Guess you can't aim so well in the dark.*

No wonder it had taken the guy so many hits to crash the SUV.

But the man hadn't given up. He'd kept shooting and—

"You should never have touched Ava!" The other words had been a rasp, but those were a scream. "She was mine. She was waiting for me! And you ruined everything!" A high, sharp scream.

Mark ducked behind a tree. He swiped his hand over his eyes to get rid of the blood that slid down from his forehead. He had his makeshift weapon. Now he just needed to find the right moment to attack.

Then he heard the growl of an engine. One that wasn't coming from his ranch but instead seemed to be coming from the main road—the road from the Mc-Guire ranch.

Ava's coming. She thinks she's coming to find you…

His phone had been missing from the SUV. The driver's side door had been open… That guy must have used it to contact Ava! He'd lured her in with Mark as the bait.

Now he was waiting out there, armed with a gun, and Ava would have no clue what kind of hell she was walking into tonight.

I can't let him hurt her!

He heard the thud of footsteps. His attacker was moving, probably rushing to better ground so that he could attack Ava when she approached. He'd fired at Mark's vehicle, sending him crashing. The guy was planning the same kind of attack on Ava.

No! Mark left his cover and ran after the attacker. Mark could see his shadowy form moving fast. The guy was rushing toward the road and the approaching vehicle.

"She isn't yours!" Mark yelled out.

The other man froze. Then he started to swing around to face Mark.

Mark tackled him. They hit the ground, and the attacker's gun flew from his fingers. Mark brought his weapon up and put it against the man's neck. He definitely had on a ski mask, one that completely shielded his face, but his neck was open, and the glass pressed to his skin. "Make another move," Mark snarled at him, "and you're a dead man."

The growl of the engine was coming closer and closer.

But the guy just laughed. "Left...a little surprise for sweet Ava." His voice was a rasp. "Won't ever see it coming."

Mark's head whipped up. It was so dark. He could only see the flash of Ava's headlights as she drove—too fast—toward his ranch. "What did you do?"

And then he saw the headlights swirl. They spun around as the car seemed to lose control.

"I left some spikes in the road for Ava."

He heard a crash, and terror clawed inside Mark's chest.

"I didn't want her getting to you too fast," that rasping voice told him.

Mark slammed the guy's head into the ground, and the masked man's body seemed to go limp. Mark jumped to his feet and roared, "Ava!" as he started running toward the crash. Pain and fear twisted through him. He had to get to her, to find her. He pushed himself to run faster. Pushed so he could *get to Ava*. She'd been coming to help him, and if she was hurt, he didn't know what in the hell he would do.

His feet thudded over the earth. His breath heaved out. Ava. He had to reach Ava.

"Freeze!"

And suddenly a bright light was shining on him.

"Mark?" That was Ava's voice, coming from behind the light. "He's bleeding!"

Yeah, he was probably bleeding from about a dozen different spots. So what? Ava was there—she was alive. She was also running to him. He could see her clearly now. She threw herself against him and embraced him. "I was so worried," she whispered.

The bright light was still on him, and Mark squinted, trying to see past it, even as he held Ava as tightly as he could.

"What is happening?" a sharp voice demanded—Davis's voice. He was the one with the light, and as he approached, Mark realized Davis was also holding a gun.

Brodie was at his twin's side. "Someone put spikes in the road," Brodie muttered.

"He's back there," Mark said, pointing behind him. "I left him on the ground." Each word seemed to take way too much effort, and the blood was dripping in his eyes again.

But Ava is safe. She's in my arms. I won't let anything happen to her.

"He...shot at me when I drove through the gate. Crashed, and he was waiting..."

"Where is he?" Davis demanded.

"About fifteen feet in front...of the line of trees... west side..."

Davis took off running with his gun drawn. Brodie was a step behind him.

Mark didn't join the hunt. He wasn't about to leave Ava. His hand curled around her chin. "I heard the crash," he whispered. "Baby, are you okay?"

"I'm not the one bleeding all over the place," she said. "We have to get you to a hospital."

Yeah, he could probably use some stitches—or maybe a few dozen. But... "I was scared," he told her, the words little more than a growl. "Knew he was... going after you. Can't let him...can't let him hurt you."

"And I didn't want him hurting you!" Her voice was sharp. She pulled out her phone and called 9-1-1. As she talked, Ava kept one hand on him, almost as if she was afraid of letting him go.

He knew he couldn't let her go. Ava mattered too much.

DAVIS'S LIGHT SWEPT over the battered remains of Mark's SUV. The windshield was gone, and bullet holes littered the vehicle.

Behind him, Brodie gave a low whistle. "Someone was playing hard."

"He wasn't playing." His backed away from the vehicle. It was so dark out there, and the light he was shining made him a target. He'd searched where Mark indicated, but there had been so sign of the man who'd tried to kill Mark. He and Brodie had branched out and scanned the area, but the guy had seemingly vanished.

"He didn't realize just how hard Mark would be to take down." Davis killed his light. He wanted to get back to Ava and Mark just in case the man they were searching for had decided to circle around for another attack. "His mistake."

Because Davis knew just how Mark had spent his years away from Austin. He'd kept secrets for Mark over the years, just as Mark had kept quiet about Davis's past. There were some things that shouldn't be shared.

The world already had enough nightmares.

He and Brodie hurried back to Ava. There were too many trees around them. Too many places to vanish. He hadn't heard the sound of a car, so the guy they were hunting must still be on foot.

If he was lying in wait out here, then he must know the area. To vanish so quickly in the dark, he has to be familiar with this land.

There were some old trails leading away from Mark's ranch. The guy could've escaped on one of those and had a ride waiting in the distance.

Or the man could still be out there, hiding and waiting for a chance to take another shot at his prey.

You won't get a shot at my sister. No one messed with his family. No one.

When he got back to Mark and Ava, he wasn't surprised to see that Mark had moved them closer to Brodie's smashed car. They'd hit the side of a tree after going over those spikes, but the body of the vehicle was still rock solid. Mark and Ava had taken shelter back there.

"I called the ranch," Mark muttered to him. "Help's on the way. Until the cops get here, my men can hold that jerk who—"

"We didn't see him." But they had found a gun the guy had left behind. He'd tucked it into his waistband so he could give it to the cops.

"He's still out there?" Mark demanded, and Davis saw Mark instantly pull Ava closer to him.

He'd known how Mark felt about Ava. When the guy looked at her, his eyes always got that too-intense expression in them. But Mark had been keeping his hands off Ava for years. He'd stayed away.

Looks like he's not holding back any longer.

Instead, he was holding her tight.

Davis knew that any man who tried to take Ava from Mark Montgomery would have a fight on his hands.

"I'm not like Gregory." No, Mark wasn't, but he was still one very dangerous man. How would Ava respond when she learned about Mark's past?

He heard the approach of vehicles then—several, by the sound of things. The cars weren't coming from the main road. Instead, they were coming from the Montgomery ranch. Had to be Mark's staff, rushing to help. Good. He could use them. They could fan out and search the area. Because if that guy was still close— *and he has to be*—then they still had a chance of stopping him.

The vehicles braked. Car doors slammed. The men hurried forward.

"Mark, buddy, are you okay?" Davis recognized the voice of Ty Watts, Mark's foreman and friend.

"He's not okay," Ava said, her voice shaking. "He's bleeding too much, and the ambulance needs to hurry."

Davis tensed. He hadn't examined Mark's wounds because the guy had looked strong when he ran toward them. But Mark was an ex-soldier. If he was at death's door, he'd still probably race straight ahead, showing no weakness.

"We need your men to search," Davis said, his words sharp. "We have a man out there, possibly armed." He didn't know how many guns the guy might have brought to the ambush. "He was here a few minutes ago, and we have to find him."

Before he decided to attack again.

Brodie led the men on the search.

Davis slapped his hand on Mark's shoulder. "How bad?" he asked softly.

"I've had much worse."

Davis noticed that Mark's hand was still wrapped around Ava's as if he couldn't bear to let her go.

"We'll get him," Davis assured him before he started to turn away.

But Mark's words stopped him.

"I should have killed him," Mark muttered, "when I had the chance."

"No!" came Ava's instant denial. "Mark, you're not a killer. That's not who you—"

Mark's laughter was bitter as he finally eased his hold on Ava. "Oh, baby, there is so much you don't know about me."

"Mark?" Now her voice was hesitant.

"Next time," Mark promised, the words heavy with lethal certainty, "he won't walk away. He's not going to have you, no matter what that sick freak thinks."

Davis tensed.

"He said you're his, Ava." Mark seemed to be gritting out the words. "He thinks he's going to have you."

An obsession. One that had sure escalated tonight.

"I don't—" Ava began.

"He told me…that he had plans for you. That he'd had plans since…" Mark's voice roughened, and he stopped.

Mark was holding back. They couldn't afford that.

"What did the guy say?" Davis prompted Mark.

Mark's hand lifted as if he'd touch Ava again, but then his hand fell back to his side and his fingers clenched into a fist. "I'm sorry, Ava."

This wasn't good.

"Mark?" Fear threaded through his name as Ava reached out—and she didn't hesitate. She touched Mark. She curled her fingers around his hand and held tight.

"He said…" In the distance, Davis could finally hear the faint sound of an ambulance approaching. "He said he'd had plans for you…ever since you were sixteen…"

MARK MONTGOMERY WASN'T DEAD.

He was still very much *alive* and the man was currently with Ava. *With my Ava!*

And Ava…she'd been bad. He'd told her to come to him. She should have come alone, but instead, she'd brought her brothers with her. Those two McGuire men had leapt out of the vehicle with their guns in their hands. They'd been searching so desperately near the crash scene. They'd almost—*almost!*—seen him. They'd found one of his guns. Luckily he'd been wearing gloves so there wouldn't be any fingerprints on the weapon. They *shouldn't* be able to trace it back to him, but…

He eased deeper into the shadows. Men were searching all around the area. But there were so many dark spots hidden beneath the trees. He'd prepared well for this night. He'd learned the area far better than anyone else. He knew how to disappear.

And I know how to bide my time.

Because he would have to wait for Mark to lower his guard once more. Then he'd attack. Mark Montgomery wasn't going to get away from him.

As he watched, Ava reached out. Her fingers curled around Mark's as if…as if she just had to touch him.

No, Ava, he's not for you!

Ava had to understand. She would never be with Mark. Mark was a dead man walking. The guy just didn't know it yet.

But you will, Mark.

Mark had never belonged there. He and that sick bastard Gregory Montgomery had no right to that land. They weren't worthy.

He'd taken everything away from Gregory. At the end, the old fool had begged. He'd promised the world to him.

But it hadn't mattered. He'd killed Gregory, and no one had even known. Gregory hadn't been his first kill and wouldn't be his last. Any people who got in his way—they would all be eliminated.

I will take what I want.

And the thing he wanted most…was Ava. Sweet, beautiful Ava. He'd already done so much for her. Did she even realize it? Did she even know?

I killed for you, Ava. And I'll do it again and again.

THE EMTS WERE dragging Mark into the back of an ambulance. He was trying to stay, despite the fact that he was bleeding all over the place.

"Ava!" Mark tried to push toward her.

"Go with him," Davis told her as he gave her shoulder a quick squeeze. "I'll keep searching here."

She moved forward, her body feeling numb. Mark's words kept replaying in her head. *He said he'd had plans for you...ever since you were sixteen...*

Nausea was rolling inside her as she climbed into the back of that ambulance. Mark finally settled down then, and he let the EMTs start checking out his body.

There was so much blood on him. Dripping from a gash on his forehead, coming from scrapes and cuts on his arm—

"Looks like a bullet grazed you here," one of the EMTs murmured as he studied Mark's right shoulder.

"I just need a few stitches," Mark told him. "I'll be fine. Check Ava—her car crashed, too! You need to make sure she's okay."

"I'm fine," Ava said. "And it wasn't my car—it was Brodie's." She was fine, physically. But her mind was a wreck right then. This man after her—if he'd been making plans since she was sixteen, had he been one of the men who killed her parents? Had they truly died because of her?

Her fingers were shaking. She looked out the back of the ambulance and saw Davis staring at her. His expression was hard, angry. Did he blame her, too?

Davis slammed those back doors shut. The ambulance's siren screamed as the vehicle lurched forward.

"Sir, how many fingers am I holding up?" Ava heard the EMT ask Mark.

"Two, and get 'em out of my way." His response was a snarl. "Ava? Ava, you're trembling!"

And she was. She'd slid back into a corner of the ambulance, hoping to make room for the EMTs to work, but heavy tremors were running through her body. "He tried to kill you," she whispered.

One of the EMTs turned toward her. "Ma'am? Ma'am, where do you hurt?"

In her heart...

"He was attacking you because of me." She knew it.

Mark gave her a grim smile. "Baby, I'm a hard man to kill."

That didn't make her feel any better. In fact, his low words, spoken in a hard voice that she'd never heard from him before, just made her feel even worse. Because she realized right then—*I don't know Mark nearly as well as I thought.*

His blue eyes had turned cold and icy, and for a moment, she almost felt as if she were staring into the gaze of a stranger.

Chapter Six

They hadn't found the man who'd attacked him. Mark had talked to the cops. He'd repeated his story at least four times to them.

But he hadn't seen the man's face. He hadn't recognized that low, rasping voice. He knew the guy had been close to his own height and that he had been well muscled. He suspected the man was familiar with the area because he had known just where to wait for his ambush—and he'd been able to disappear so quickly. But other than that, he hadn't been able to give the cops much information at all.

He's a psycho and he'd obsessed with Ava. Those had been Mark's words to the cops. Ava had stood there, far too pale and far too tense, during the interview with the police. *He said I wouldn't have her. That she was his.*

Ava had actually flinched when he said those words.

She'd spoken very little. And when they'd left the hospital, she'd seemed to withdraw completely from him. Now he was in the vehicle with her and Davis, heading back to his ranch, and he was—what? Just supposed to leave Ava?

There were at least a few more hours before dawn.

With that maniac still on the loose out there, he didn't want to let Ava out of his sight.

She was in the front seat with Davis. She hadn't looked back at Mark, not even once. *What is happening?*

He leaned forward. "Don't bother going to my ranch tonight. I already talked to Ty. He'll have extra security out there."

Now Ava did slant him a quick glance. Finally.

"Take me to Ava's place," he said flatly. And Davis had better not even try arguing with him. After everything that had happened, he wouldn't be separated from her.

"You think you're spending the night with my sister?" Davis asked him. Apparently, he *was* going to try arguing.

"I think I'm going to be your sister's guard until dawn." Because Ava would be scared and because— fine, *he* was the one who was scared. Scared that the man out there might attack Ava again when Mark wasn't close. What would he do then?

"Brodie and I can watch Ava." Davis's voice was flat. "You need to rest."

Right. Like he'd be able to rest with the adrenaline rush still coursing through his veins. "I let him get away," he said. "I should have—"

"Don't." Ava's voice was brittle. "Don't even say it, do you understand?" And she turned to glare at him. "Don't say that you should have killed him. That's not you. That's not what you do! You don't kill people! You help—you save people, just like you saved me!"

Not always, Ava.

"You know I can keep her safe," Mark said. Davis

was one of the few people who knew all about his past. "Don't you want as much protection for her as possible?"

He saw Davis give a grim nod. Good, because if Davis had taken Mark back to the Montgomery ranch, he just would have forced his way back inside the McGuire place.

The rest of the ride passed in silence. The road was pitch black. Mark kept glancing around, hyperaware now that threats could come at any time. Until that guy was caught, he knew he'd be looking over his shoulder.

And trying to keep Ava as close as possible.

Davis took them through the big gates at the Mc-Guire ranch. The vehicle eased up the drive until they got to the guest cottage. Ava hurriedly jumped out of the car, and Davis followed her.

Mark exited, but he stood back a minute, waiting to see what went down between Ava and her brother.

"You should stay up at the main house," Davis told Ava. "Jennifer got a room ready for you—you know you'll be safe there."

"I'm starting to think no one is safe...anywhere."

Mark had to strain in order to hear her words.

"Come to the main house," Davis said again.

But Ava shook her head. "I'm staying here with Mark."

Yes.

Davis turned toward him. "You see anything suspicious, you call me, got it? You sound an alarm, and you get me here."

If he saw an attack coming, Mark would be striking back with all the power that he had.

Davis paced toward him. He leaned in close. His

voice no more than a breath of sound, he warned Mark, "And you keep your hands off my sister, got it?"

No, he didn't. Mark grabbed Davis's arm, stopping him before he could leave. Keeping his voice just as low as Davis's had been, Mark said, "Ava's an adult. What happens between us…it's just between *us*." If Ava wanted him, the last thing he'd do would be to turn away from her.

Davis could get angry. The guy could try to take a swing at Mark, but there was no way Mark was staying away from Ava. Not now.

Davis's expression was unreadable in the darkness. But when he said, "You hurt her, and I'll break you," Mark understood his threat.

Then Davis was heading back to the car.

Ava had opened the door to her cottage. Mark rushed forward, not wanting her to go in alone. He caught her hand. "Let me check it out."

"The…the alarm's still on. The place should be safe."

It should be, but he still wanted to check in there. Mark hurried inside and did a sweep of the guest house. The den was clear. So was the kitchen, the bathroom, the bedroom and—

He opened another door. The room there was mostly empty except for about a dozen canvases that had been stacked near the walls.

"No one here but us," Ava said, her voice still sounding brittle. Sharp. Not at all like Ava. "I told you the place was safe."

He turned to look at her, but Ava's eyes were on the canvases. "I store them here because I don't want anyone else to see them." She seemed to hesitate. Then she said, "Maybe I should just throw them out."

He'd never seen Ava's paintings before. He didn't think anyone had. He took a step toward those canvases.

This time, she was the one to reach out to him.

"We all have...secrets, don't we?"

Yes.

Her gaze rose to hold his. "Who are you?"

Mark shook his head, not understanding.

"Are you the man who kept me sane all those years ago? The white knight, riding to my rescue?" She swallowed. The faint click of sound was almost painful to hear. "Or are you the guy who talks about killing a man in a way...in a way that makes me think you'd really do it? That you wouldn't hesitate at all?"

Her fingers were so soft against his skin. Like silk. "If your life was on the line, I wouldn't hesitate." He would do anything for her.

Who are you?

"I'm both men." Good and bad tangled together.

Ava was so close to him. Her gaze searched his. "Should I be afraid of you?"

He shook his head. "I won't hurt you." It was a vow he'd made to himself long ago.

"Can I trust you?"

There were things she didn't know, but when it came to her safety... "Yes."

Ava glanced back toward the canvases. He couldn't see what she'd painted on them, and he wanted to stride forward.

But he also wanted her to keep touching him.

"You told the police that the man who attacked you said I was his."

His back teeth clenched. "Yes."

"What do you think he'll do...to me?"

If he had the chance… The image flashed in Mark's mind, and rage burned inside him.

"That's what I think, too," Ava said, seeming to read Mark's thoughts. "Why? Why does he want to hurt me? I don't even know him."

He wrapped his arms around her shoulders and pulled her against him. "Because he's sick, Ava. You didn't do anything. It's this guy. He's just—"

"If he started making plans when I was sixteen, then do you think… Was he one of the men who killed my parents?"

Mark was afraid that he just might be.

"Why?" Her head titled back as she stared up at him. "Why is he doing this? Why is he focusing on me?"

"I don't know." He wished he had words to comfort her.

Her gaze slid over his face, then up to his forehead. The docs had put in a few stitches there, and they'd stitched up his shoulder. The wounds didn't hurt him. He'd had much worse before, courtesy of Gregory and the life he'd led after leaving the ranch.

"I'm sorry he hurt you." She stood on her tiptoes and pressed a light kiss to his cheek. "The people I care about always seem to get hurt because of me."

Her scent teased him. Strawberries. Ava.

He closed his eyes as he just drank her in for a moment.

"I'll…get some covers for you. You can sleep on the couch. Or, I mean, if you want, you can take the bed."

He opened his eyes.

"You're the one who was hurt," she whispered. "I can easily bunk on the couch while you take the bed."

He'd rather be in that bed with her.

"I heard the doctors…" She exhaled softly. "They said you might have a concussion. Is it even safe for you to sleep—"

"I'm not planning to sleep." Too much adrenaline pumped through him. He wouldn't be sleeping any-time soon. "And you…you take the bed, Ava. I'll be fine on the couch."

She nodded and slipped from the room. Her soft footsteps padded away.

He stared at the stack of canvases. Ava had made those, and because they were hers…part of Ava…he found himself striding across that room. He wondered what she would paint. When she'd been in her early teens, she'd always taken a sketchbook around the ranch with her. He'd found the sketchbook once. It had been filled with drawings of her horse, her brothers. Even… *Me.*

He'd been blown away by her work. It was so beau-tiful and detailed for someone so young. What would her work be like now?

He picked up the first canvas.

Mark sucked in a sharp breath.

Her work…it was still beautiful. But it was dark. She wasn't sketching anything anymore. Not painting horses or people. The art was abstract. Angry reds and turbulent grays. He picked up more canvases, going through them, seeing the same emotions jumping out at him again and again.

Rage.

Pain.

They were twisted together in her paintings, so strong he could feel the emotions battering at him as he gazed at her work. So strong that—

The last canvas was a painting of a man. Ava's father. He was staring back from that canvas, his eyes filled with fear even as his face was twisted with rage.

The floor creaked. Mark's head snapped up. Ava stood in the doorway. She had a pillow and a blanket in her arms. She gazed at him, her eyes wide. Hurt.

"Ava—"

"Not so beautiful anymore, are they?"

He didn't speak. The paintings *were* beautiful. In a dark and almost unearthly way.

"You told me once that my sketches were beautiful."

He put down the last canvas and took a step toward her.

"When I pick up a brush now, it's all so…rough." She gave a hard shake of her head. "It was supposed to be therapeutic, doing that. At least, that's what I read in one of those crazy self-help books. 'Paint your emotions.' But I guess I didn't realize my emotions were so violent."

Because there was violence in her work.

"I…want them to pay."

He took another step toward her.

"I want the men who killed my parents to suffer. I want them to hurt, just like I hurt." Her voice dropped. "My brothers want to shut me out and hunt these men on their own, but…it's about me. Don't they get that? I was there. My father's last moments—he was staring right at me."

With fear in his eyes and rage on his face.

"I won't be shut out." Her laughter held a desperate edge. "Especially since I know they died because of me." She pushed the pillow and the blanket into his arms. Then she spun on her heel.

"It wasn't because of you." He wanted to be clear on that.

She looked back over her shoulder. "But that man tonight—"

"If he was involved, that has nothing to do with you. You didn't ask him to kill your parents."

Ava flinched. That *had* been one of the vicious rumors circulated about her. That she'd hired men to kill her parents. That they hadn't approved of her secret lover and she'd had them killed. How else had she escaped that night? Ava must have been involved. At least, that was what the gossip said.

He'd hated those stories. Every time he'd heard those tales, he'd jumped to Ava's defense. And when a few fools in a bar had been dumb enough to mouth off about Ava and her parents, Mark had started a bar fight that wound up costing him over five thousand dollars in repair fees. He'd torn that place down because those drunks had been raging about her.

They didn't even know her. Ava would never do something like that.

Because Ava... She was one of the few good things left in the world. In *his* world, he sometimes thought she might be the only good thing left.

"You didn't do this," he said again, because he wanted Ava to believe that.

"I want to give them justice. Sometimes I think if I can just get them justice—" her smile was bittersweet "—maybe I'll be able to sleep without them haunting me."

Then Ava slipped away.

AVA LAY IN BED and stared up at the ceiling. Mark was just outside the bedroom. She'd heard him getting settled for the night. Moving quietly, but the creaking floor had given him away.

Now there was only silence from the den.

She'd been so afraid earlier. So terrified that she wouldn't get to him in time.

Her fingers curled around the sheets. Mark could have died that night. And what would her life have been like then?

You have to keep going. Davis had told her that after they'd buried their parents. *We can't crawl into the ground with them. You think they'd want that? No, they'd want you to live and to be happy.*

She pushed aside the covers. She'd changed into a pair of loose shorts and a T-shirt before she'd climbed into bed.

If Mark had been killed, everyone would have expected her to soldier on.

They wouldn't have realized that her heart had been cut out of her chest.

What am I waiting for?

Ava crept toward her bedroom door. The sound of her breathing seemed far too loud to her. Her fingers touched the doorknob. She turned it and the door opened with a little squeak.

The den was dark, but her eyes quickly adjusted. She could see Mark on the sofa. Not lying down but sitting up. She inched forward.

"Did you have a bad dream, Ava?"

In a sense, yes.

"It's all right," he told her softly. "You know nightmares can't hurt you."

She stood in her doorway and tried to keep her backbone straight. "There's...there's plenty of room in the bed." She sucked in a quick breath. "There's enough space for us both. You don't have to stay on that couch."

Silence.

Her cheeks burned. As far as seduction routines went, hers was extremely lame. It was just that this moment mattered so much to her. No, *he* mattered.

"Ava..." he said her name like a caress, and she shivered in the dark. "Are you inviting me into your bed?"

"Yes." That was exactly what she was doing.

She saw his shadowy form rise. He walked toward her, big and menacing in the darkness. She didn't back away when he approached. This time, there was no hesitation. Life was too short to waste on doubts.

"Let's be very clear." His voice held an edge she couldn't quite interpret. Desire was there. Demand, really, but...more. "Are you offering me a place to sleep..."

She waited.

"Or are you offering me more?"

Ava reached out, took his hand and laced her fingers with his. "I'm offering you everything."

His fingers tightened around hers. "There won't be any going back once we cross this line."

"There's no other place that I want to go."

She turned and led him back into the bedroom. Her heart was racing in her chest, and she wondered if he could feel the nervous tremor in her fingers. She wanted to appear sophisticated and in control, but the truth was that her knees felt like jelly. This moment with him—it mattered so much to her.

"I was waiting for you," he said.

She stopped at the bed and turned back toward him. "Waited so long...for you...to come to me." His left hand rose and sank into her hair. He tipped her head back, and his head lowered toward hers. "I thought I'd go insane from waiting."

And she hadn't even thought he really wanted her, not until that kiss at his ranch.

"Is it safe?" Ava asked, a fast worry pushing through her. "With your stitches?"

"What stitches?" Then he was kissing her. Softly at first, then harder, deeper. "I don't feel a thing but you," he said against her mouth.

And *he* was all *she* could feel as he surrounded her with his strength. His chest was bare, and when he pulled her closer, his muscles flexed against her.

Her mouth opened more for him. His tongue slipped past her lips, and her hands rose to grip his shoulders.

"No interruptions this time," he said. "Just you and just me."

She moved a bit to the side, and her knees hit the mattress.

"Just you," she repeated. "Just me."

His hands curled around her hips, and he lifted her onto the bed.

Ava caught the hem of her shirt, hesitated only about half a second—because this was Mark!—and pulled the shirt over her head.

She thought that Mark was going to come closer to her then. That she'd feel his touch. Instead, the bedside lamp flashed on. She blinked against the light and saw Mark standing there, his hand still near the lamp but his eyes on her.

"You really thought…I'd take you in the dark?" He shook his head. "No, baby, I want to see everything, because I'm never forgetting you."

His gaze slid over her body, down to her breasts. Her nipples were tight and aching for him. She wanted him to touch them. She wanted him to lick them.

Mark drew in a deep breath. "Take off the shorts."

She eased back onto the bed until she was lying down. With her eyes still on him, Ava arched her hips and pushed the shorts over her hips and down her legs. When the shorts were near her knees, Mark caught them, easing the material the rest of the way off.

He dropped the shorts onto the floor. His gaze was on her underwear, a pair of black cotton panties. She wore nothing else.

"You are the sexiest thing I've ever seen."

He said the words as if he meant them. She knew Mark had probably been with plenty of lovers—he had money and power, and the guy was pure walking sex appeal—but when he stared at her, there was such stark desire in his eyes.

Like I'm the only woman for him.

That was perfect, since he was the only man for her.

His hand lifted, and he touched her shoulder. Lightly. Carefully.

That wouldn't do.

Ava shook her head. "I want everything from you that you have to give." Passion and need and a desire that burned right through any thought of control.

Their gazes held.

"Take off your jeans," Ava ordered him.

Staring at her, he did.

Her breath came faster. If possible, the need within her built even more. Desire was raging within her blood, a heat that flooded her veins.

He slid into the bed with her and kissed her, not carefully, not softly—wildly. Hard and fierce and deep, and it was exactly what she wanted from him.

Mark pushed her legs apart and slid his hips between her thighs, positioning himself at their juncture. He braced his arms, and then his mouth was moving down her neck. Licking and sucking and letting her feel the edge of his teeth in a sensual bite.

Down, down he went, and when his mouth closed over her nipple, Ava hissed out a breath because it felt so good. She arched toward him, demanding more. Now that this moment was here, she wanted to take all he had to give. She intended to savor every single moment of pleasure.

He kissed his way to her other breast. Light stubble coated his jaw, and it rasped lightly over her skin, heightening her sensitivity to him even more. He licked her nipple and sucked it deep into his mouth. Her hips jerked against him, a helpless reaction, and his long, thick arousal pressed to her core.

Her panties were the only thing between them. She wanted those panties gone. She'd longed to feel him inside her for too long already, and she didn't want to wait any longer. "Mark, *now.*"

But he was kissing her stomach. Working his way down her body and caressing her with constant touches that were driving her to the very edge of reason.

He moved his body, taking away that wonderful aroused flesh, and she cried out in frustration.

"Don't worry, baby. I'll take care of you."

Then he was touching her through the thin fabric of her panties. Stroking her, but it wasn't enough. Not even close. She needed him too much right then, and she heard herself demand, "More!"

He bent and put his mouth on the panties.

She nearly came off the bed. "Mark!"

He jerked the panties down, and she heard the faint rip of the fabric. Then he was sliding his fingers against her sex and into her. She bit her lip because the feelings were so strong. But she didn't want just to be touched by his hand. She wanted him—all of him.

"So beautiful," Mark whispered. "So perfect for me…"

She was going crazy. "Don't make me wait," she told him. She'd waited long enough. "Now, Mark, now!"

He pulled away from her, and she cried out in frustration, but he was just reaching for his jeans to grab his wallet. She realized he'd brought protection with him.

Talk about being prepared. Another thing she adored about him.

In seconds he was back. She parted her legs eagerly. He positioned his shaft at the entrance to her body, and his fingers threaded with hers. She stared into his eyes as he thrust deep.

The pain was fast. A quick burn that was lost in the tide of pleasure, but Mark's eyes went wide. "Ava?" Shock was there, and he tried to pull back.

She wasn't about to let him go. Ava locked her legs around his hips and arched toward him. He was filling her completely. She was on the edge of her release, and she just needed—

He kissed her. Hot, deep, just the way she liked.

Then he withdrew and thrust back into her. The bed seemed to shake beneath her. Again and again he thrust. Her head tipped back as the pleasure lashed through her. Ava's release was so close. So—

His hand pulled from hers. His fingers slid between

their bodies and then he was stroking her, pushing right against the center of her need. He thrust and caressed and her climax rolled over her. Ava's body shuddered as the waves seemed to consume her with so much pleasure that she lost her breath. She could only hang on to Mark and enjoy that wild, sweet ride. Her heartbeat was drumming in her ears, a thunderous rhythm, and her body was slick and sated beneath him.

He was still moving within her, thrusting deeper, harder, and making aftershocks of pleasure course through Ava. Another thrust—

His eyes seemed to go blind as he stared down at her. The darkness of his pupils spread, covering the blue of his gaze. He jerked within her, growled out her name as an expression of pure pleasure swept over his face.

Her body shivered beneath his. He was all around her. Strong and warm. And when he slowly pulled out of her body, Ava whispered a protest because she didn't want the pleasure to end.

"I'll be right back. Promise."

The mattress shifted when he rose and padded to the bathroom. Ava stretched, her muscles aching and her body feeling so incredibly good. Her eyes started to drift closed, and then she felt the soft, wet warmth of a cloth between her legs.

"Was there something you wanted to tell me?" He moved the cloth, then eased back into bed with her.

Exhaustion was pulling at Ava. She smiled and told him, "I want to make love with you again. Soon." Because he'd sure been worth waiting for.

"Ava." He said her name with a tenderness she hadn't heard before. "Did I hurt you?"

With her eyes closed, she shook her head.

"You...you should've told me that you hadn't... not before..."

He sounded so flustered that she forced her eyes to lift. "What did it matter?"

"Ava..."

She smiled at him. "I wanted you, Mark. I didn't ask who you'd been with before, and you didn't ask me, either."

"You *hadn't* been with anyone."

"Because I haven't trusted anyone else, not the way I trust you." That was the simple truth. She didn't trust him just with her body. She trusted him with her heart. Did he even realize that?

"You should have told me. *I* should have asked! I should have—"

He looked so cute and confused. She kissed him. "It was wonderful."

His hand sank into her hair. "You were wonderful."

She pulled him down beside her. "Stay with me." It just seemed natural to say those words to him. After the day they'd had—the night—she wanted to sleep with him.

His arms curled around her. She could hear the drumming of his heart beneath her ear. That strong drumming was the last sound she heard before she slipped into her dreams.

MARK MONTGOMERY WAS spending the night with Ava.

He hadn't stayed at the hospital. He hadn't returned to his ranch. He was with *her*.

Fury surged within him. He'd told Mark that Ava was his. The fool should have listened.

Mark had put up much more of a fight than he'd

anticipated. He'd thought the guy would be so easy to take out, just like Gregory had been. Gregory had been so easy. The fool had been drunk, no match for him at all. Gregory had tried to fight—too late—but there had been no point.

One blast of his gun, and he'd been done. Then all he'd needed to do was set the scene to make it look like a suicide. The cops hadn't questioned Gregory's death. Mark hadn't questioned it.

He figured everyone had just been glad the old man was dead.

He stared out into the night, so quiet and still. Ava was behind the heavy gates and security at the McGuire ranch, but she couldn't stay there forever. And Mark—he wouldn't be at Ava's side every moment. He would have to leave her sometime.

There would be a moment when Ava wasn't guarded. A moment when he could move in...

Then she truly would be his.

Mark won't take you from me. No one will. Ava had finally come back home. He wasn't going to lose her now.

Chapter Seven

When Ava opened her eyes, Mark was gone. She sat up quickly, her gaze flying around the room. She'd crashed, hard, and for the first time in longer than she could remember, she didn't know if nightmares had haunted her.

She couldn't remember anything about her dreams.

As she gazed around that room, the only thing she knew for certain was that... *I'm alone.*

Swallowing, she rose from the bed and made her way toward the bathroom. She hurried into the shower, and a quick jerk of her wrist sent the hot water powering down on her. Ava put her head under the stream, letting the water soak her hair.

Mark is gone.

What had she expected? Honestly, Ava didn't know. She hadn't thought much past the passion of the moment with him. She'd just wanted to grab on to him, wanted to hold tight and see if reality would be any match for her fantasies.

Reality had rocked. But she hadn't thought about the morning after.

A burst of cold air hit her, and Ava whirled around. The shower door had been opened and Mark—Mark was standing there, staring at her. He was dressed in jeans and a T-shirt. His hair was tousled, and his eyes seemed to be eating her alive.

The water kept pounding down on her. He kept staring at her. Yes, he definitely had the look of a starving man.

Ava's fingers flew out and turned off the rush of the water. The *drip-drip-drip* seemed incredibly loud in that moment. "I thought you'd gone."

A faint line appeared between his brows.

She was so not sounding sophisticated and cool. But sophisticated and cool were incredibly hard to do when a woman was standing naked in the shower, dripping wet, and her lover was fully clothed in front of her.

"I made you breakfast," he said, his voice gruff.

Her lips parted in surprise. He'd cooked for her? That was…nice.

"But the food's going to have to wait," he muttered and he stepped into the shower. She automatically glanced down and saw that he wasn't fully dressed, after all. His feet were bare—

He kissed her. Mark pushed her back against the tiled wall, and his mouth took hers. This wasn't a getting-to-know-you sort of kiss. They were far, *far* past that stage. When his lips touched hers, she felt as if he were claiming her. Only fair—she definitely wanted to claim him. Her wet hands grabbed for his shirt, and she shoved it up and out of her way. She wanted to touch him, skin to skin. The press of his lips against hers had ignited a firestorm of desire within her.

His hands were sliding over her body, caressing her breasts and stroking her aching nipples. Then down, down his hand went. She was slick from the shower, and he pushed his hand between the folds of her sex.

Ava rose onto her tiptoes, gasping because his touch felt so good.

Everything about Mark felt right.

"Am I...hurting you?" He seemed to force out the words.

She pressed a kiss to his neck. Bit him, then licked the skin. "Only if you stop..." Because the pleasure had risen so quickly.

Her left hand jerked open the snap of his jeans.

"I've got...protection."

Good. because she wanted him, right then.

A few moments later, he was lifting her up against that wall, holding her easily as he drove inside her. The wall was cold and hard behind her, and he was hot and strong before her. *In* her.

He was lifting her up against him, then bringing her down, and every stroke, every move had her desire swelling even more. Her breath panted out, her heartbeat drummed like mad in her ears and her nails dug into his back.

"I love the way you feel," Mark whispered right before he kissed her again. "So perfect...like you were made for me."

The release hit her. Even harder than before. Deeper, longer, and Ava tried to muffle the sound of her scream.

Mark was with her. She felt his aroused flesh jerk within her, and the contractions of her inner muscles seemed to push him over the edge. But he didn't muffle his cry. He roared her name, and then he held her so tight.

So tight she wondered if he'd ever let her go.

BREAKFAST WAS A cold, soggy mess. Not that it had been much better *before* he'd seen Ava in the shower and pretty much lost his mind. The eggs were runny, and the toast—well, maybe the toast was still edible. Maybe. And—

"You didn't have to cook for me."

Ava's voice had him turning around. She stood just a few feet away. Fully dressed now—unfortunately— in a pair of jeans and a white T-shirt. She'd pulled her hair back into a ponytail, and her skin gleamed. She gave him a smile, one that showed her gorgeous dimples. "But thank you."

He smiled back at her. Ava just made him feel... good. "I don't think you should thank me, not until you actually taste the food."

She laughed. He loved that light and sweet sound. Her laughter was far too rare, and just to hear it right then, he felt as if he'd won the lottery.

Ava headed over to the little table. She sat down and actually reached for those runny eggs. He caught her wrist. "Don't." He sighed. "Baby, this stuff has to taste like garbage."

She laughed. "Yes, I'm pretty sure it does."

He stared into her eyes. The green was gleaming. Her cheeks were flushed a light pink and her full lips curved. She didn't look like a woman who'd been beaten by life. She looked—*perfect*.

"Ava—" he began.

But there was a knock at the front door.

"That's probably Davis," she said.

Or Brodie. Either man equaled trouble. Because Ava's neck was a little red from where his stubble had chaffed her. Her lips were swollen from his kiss, and it was going to be obvious to her brothers that Mark had not kept his hands off her.

He wondered who would throw the first punch. He knew from past experience that Davis had a killer right hook.

Ava rose and headed for the door. Mark followed her, and when the door opened, he braced himself. Sure enough, Davis was waiting on the threshold.

Big surprise.

Davis's gaze—a harder green than Ava's—raked over her. That glittering stare immediately turned on Mark, then narrowed.

"Don't," Ava bit out when Davis opened his mouth to speak. "I've seen you with far too many lovers in your life, Davis. And I haven't ever said a word about them. So don't even think of launching into Mark right now."

Davis blinked.

"I'm the one who seduced him," Ava continued, her voice tight with anger. She even moved, placing her body right beside Mark's. "So back off."

Mark had to fight to keep the smile off face.

A muscle jerked in Davis's jaw. "There have not been that many lovers," he muttered. Then he rubbed the back of his neck. "And you're my kid sister!"

"I'm a woman. And what happens between Mark and me...that's our business."

"You're the one shouting about seducing him!" Davis pointed out.

Ava blushed, but she stood her ground. "And you're the one acting like I'm still sixteen. I'm not."

Davis backed up. "I just wanted to make sure you were both okay this morning."

Mark was feeling pretty good. He'd woken up with Ava—that was a whole lot better than his usual routine...when he woke up, wishing she was close.

"No alarms were triggered last night," Davis continued. "So I don't know if the guy just decided to lie low or if he's biding his time for a reason. Now that the sun's out, I want to head back to where you crashed and see if I can find any trace evidence the guy might have left behind. Maybe something we missed in the dark."

That sounded like a good idea to Mark.

"Can you come and walk me through things?" Davis asked him. "Show me exactly where you were when he attacked?"

Mark nodded. He wanted to walk through that area, too. He glanced over at Ava.

"You can bet I'm coming," she said quickly. "Let me just grab my bag and I'll be ready." Ava hurriedly backed away.

Mark didn't move from the doorway.

Davis held his gaze. "Remember what I said before," Davis murmured. "You hurt her…"

"I won't." Hurting Ava wasn't even a possibility for him. He'd kept his emotions locked down for so long. No one realized how he felt about Ava. He was just starting to understand the full depth of his emotions. Ava mattered—plain and simple—more than anything.

"I'm ready," Ava's voice was a little breathless. Her cheeks were flushed, and he had a quick flash of seeing her in that shower. The steam had been rising around her. Her delicate skin had been tinted pink. She'd been naked, her body wet, and she'd nearly brought him to his knees.

Did she have any clue just how much power she wielded over him?

Ava's stare met his. "Are you ready?"

To head back to the scene where someone had tried

to kill him? Mark gave her a grim smile. "Always." Because it was time to turn the tables on that guy. The stalker wasn't going to keep hunting them. It was time for him to become prey.

MARK'S WRECKED SUV had been towed away. Ava stared at the broken glass that still littered the scene and at the smashed gate. A shiver slid over her. Mark had been so lucky to walk away.

"He came to the vehicle while I was trapped inside," Mark said as he stepped over shards of glass. "He was about to shoot me, but I managed to get out before he fired off another shot."

Ava's eyes closed.

"I ran to the woods, over there, because I was trying to get to shelter."

Ava opened her eyes, exhaled and followed the men to the trees.

"I could hear another car coming—I thought it was Ava's car," Mark said, his voice deepening, "and I knew I had to act. He still had a gun, and I was afraid he'd shoot at her."

Mark had saved her again. She'd thought that she was racing to his rescue, but he'd been looking after her. Ava edged away from the men. They were searching the ground, scanning the area so carefully.

"I knocked him down here," Mark said. Ava was about ten feet away from him. "The gun flew out of his hand."

"Yeah, that's where I found the weapon." Davis hesitated. "Did you see where the guy ran off to?"

"No, I was too busy trying to get to Ava. I'd heard the crash, and I didn't know how badly she was hurt."

He turned toward her. "I just needed to get to her," he said softly.

Ava backed away, sliding closer to the line of trees and then—then she turned because she could hear the sound of a horse's hooves pounding on the earth. Mark and Davis hurried toward her just as a stallion burst out of the trees. It was Mark's horse, Legacy. And he was running fast—wild—heading straight toward her at a furious gallop.

No, no, Legacy shouldn't be there. He should be back in his stables.

"Ava!" Mark shouted.

But she'd already leapt to the side. She hit the ground, hard, but she escaped the dangerous crash of the horse's hooves as Legacy raced by her.

Mark gave a loud whistle, trying to signal the horse, but Legacy just reared back. The horse cried out—a sound like a high, sharp scream—and he raced toward Davis with a shaking head and rolling eyes.

Something is wrong with him!

"Legacy, no!" Mark yelled, his voice sharp with command.

Davis swore and dodged for cover. Like Ava, he wound up in the dirt. But the horse kept coming for him, stomping, thrashing.

There was no saddle on the animal. No reins. How had he gotten out there? Legacy was Mark's prized stallion. He should have been safe in the stables.

The horse whirled around and ran toward Ava again.

"No!" Mark was there in front of her. "Legacy." His voice held only powerful command, no anger, just deadly control. "Legacy, stop."

The horse wasn't stopping. He was—

Legacy collapsed. Just fell right there in the dirt.

Ava rushed toward him even as Mark and Davis closed in on the animal. He was sprawled in the dirt, his eyes still wild, his breathing hitching.

Mark put his hand on Legacy's chest. "His heartbeat is out of control." He gave a hard shake of his head as he stroked the animal. "Something has happened to him! This isn't—this isn't Legacy!"

White foam was forming near the animal's mouth.

Davis yanked out his phone. She heard him calling, asking to speak to Dr. Myers—she knew Jamie Myers was the veterinarian in the area who took care of the horses at both the McGuire and Montgomery ranches.

"He should be in the stables," Mark muttered. "Legacy should be secured in the stables!"

But he wasn't. He was on the ground before them, his whole body convulsing.

Ava fell to her knees beside Mark.

And Legacy's eyes closed.

"POISONED?" MARK DEMANDED as fury burned in him. "You're telling me that my horse was poisoned?"

Jamie Myers exhaled slowly. They'd managed to transport Legacy back to the Montgomery stables, but it sure hadn't been an easy task. The animal had had repeated spells of rearing and thrashing during the journey back, and Mark had barely managed to keep him controlled.

"I'll have to do more blood work to know for sure, but yes, he's exhibiting all of the signs," Jamie said with certainty. She pushed back a wisp of blond hair that had escaped from the bun at her nape. "His heartbeat is too accelerated, his breathing isn't stable and these spells he keeps having—"

Spells where the horse tried to break free.

She ran her hand over Legacy's back. "I'm going to stay with him and figure this thing out."

Jamie had been taking care of Mark's horses and the horses at the McGuire ranch for the past year, ever since she'd come into the area, seeming a bit out of place in her fancy clothes but more than ready to get her hands dirty as she worked on the animals.

Jamie had come from the Northeast. She never talked about her family, and from what Mark had been able to tell, she didn't get too close with many people.

He respected that about her. She was a woman with secrets.

Secrets she didn't want shared.

"He'll be okay, Mark," she promised him. "He's already getting more stabilized. It's a good thing you found him when you did. If he'd run into the road when cars were coming out this way..."

Legacy could have died. The stallion had almost run *them* down.

When it came to the ranch, Mark wasn't too sentimental about many things, but Legacy mattered. Mark and his mother had bought Legacy. Legacy was *theirs*.

The horse was the only thing of his mother's that he had left.

"I'll check all the horses," Jamie said. The faintest hint of a New England accent whispered in and out of her voice. "If any of the others are affected, I'll let you know."

He nodded. He stared across the stall at Legacy.

There was no food in the stall. The place didn't appear to have been disturbed at all.

The security feed.

If someone had come into the barn to poison Legacy, the feed would have caught it. "I'll be in the house," Mark said abruptly, "if you need me."

Jamie nodded, but her attention was on Legacy, not Mark.

He hurried out of the stall and—

"Is he okay?"

Ava was there. She'd been standing with her back propped against the side of his stables. He looked around, but he didn't see any sign of Davis.

"Mark?" Ava marched closer to him. "How's your horse?"

"Poisoned." He raked a hand through his hair. "At least, that's what the doc thinks." And he was about to figure out just who had been given access to his horse. He caught Ava's hand and hurried toward the main house.

When he stepped onto the porch, Ty rounded the corner of the house. "Boss!" Ty called out. "Boss, I got something you're gonna need to see!"

Mark glanced over at him.

Ty held up a syringe. "I just found this out back." His face darkened. "With Legacy acting so wild, I'm betting this is the cause."

Mark's jaw was clenched so tightly it hurt as he stared at that syringe. There was a thin, white label wrapped around. The name of whatever drug had been inside it? Hell, that was exactly what they needed! "Take it to Dr. Myers. She's with Legacy."

Ty nodded curtly and headed for the stables.

"Wait! Did you hear anyone last night?" Mark demanded.

Ty looked back. "I patrolled out here, but I didn't see a thing. Whoever this guy is…" Ty shook his head. His eyes hardened. "He's good. And he knows your ranch. He knows how to slip in and out without being seen by anyone."

But had he managed to avoid the video cameras?

Mark and Ava headed into the ranch house. Ava was quiet beside him as he keyed up the video feed. He fast-forwarded through the footage, watching, looking for any sign of the masked man who'd been on his property before.

You're just making yourself at home here, aren't you?

But…there was no one on the tape. No one but Ty, going in for what Mark thought must have been a quick check on the horses.

"No one's there." Ava leaned over his chair, and her hair slid over his arm. "He was too smart this time. He must've figured out where the cameras were positioned."

Maybe.

The scent of strawberries hung in the air around him.

"I know how important Legacy is to you," Ava told him as she rubbed his left shoulder. "I'm sorry this happened."

Everyone in the area knew how much he valued Legacy. "He tried to hurt me by taking him out." He looked up at her. "He could have drugged him last night after the accident."

Ava sucked in a sharp breath. "When you called your men to the scene—"

"It was the same technique he used before. Distract

and attack." The guy must have seized the opportunity. Since he hadn't been able to take out Mark, rage would have been riding the guy hard. And he'd let that rage out on Legacy.

Ava backed up when Mark stood. "He's going to be okay," she said. "Brodie has talked about Dr. Myers plenty of times. He said she knew her animals better than anyone he'd ever seen."

Yes, she did. They returned to the stables, but before they could enter, the doors swung open and Dr. Myers hurried toward them. Ty was right behind her. She smiled when she saw Mark. "He's going to be okay!" She had the syringe in a plastic bag. "I know what to give him to counteract the effects. Legacy will be fine."

Some of the heavy tension left Mark's shoulders.

"If Ty hadn't found this syringe…" She glanced over at the foreman. "Well, let's just say I'm very grateful. Now, if you'll excuse me, I need to call my office so I can get the right medicine for him." She took off jogging to her car.

Mark clapped his hand on Ty's shoulder. "I owe you."

But Ty shook his head. "No way, man. I'm the one who owes you. And we both know it's more than I can ever repay."

Mark's jaw tightened. He and Ty had become friends in school. Ty's mother had never seemed to care about her son at all. She'd seemed more interested in drinking her way to the bottom of a bottle and, most nights, Ty and Mark had hung out together. When Mark had come back to town, he'd sought out Ty. The guy had been one step away from living on the streets. He'd given Ty a place to stay and offered him a job.

Ty was one of his oldest friends—and, no, the man didn't owe him a thing.

"I'm guessing you didn't see anything on the video," Ty said, his lips twisting.

Ava stepped forward. "No one was there."

"I'll step up the guards tonight," Ty promised. "You'll be safe here."

"I'll be staying with Ava tonight," Mark said. That night, and every night until they caught the bastard.

Ty glanced over at Ava. "I sure am glad you're all right."

She gave him a weak smile. "Mark was the one who got hurt."

He'd forgotten about his stitches. They didn't matter.

Dr. Myers had returned from her car, and she was heading for the stables once more.

"Go on," Ava told Mark, pushing him forward. "Check on Legacy. I'm going to meet up with Davis."

Right. Because Davis was still searching the area near the crash.

Mark pulled her close to kiss her hard. "If you need me…"

"You'll know," she finished as she gave his arm a quick squeeze. "I'll call. But don't worry, I'll be with Davis." Then she waved a quick farewell to him and Ty.

As she walked away, Ty gave a soft whistle. "You must be feeling pretty brave to go up against all the McGuires, buddy."

Ava was worth tangling with her brothers.

"She knows," Ty began carefully, "about your past?"

His past. Those lost years when he'd slipped from Texas. "No."

"Aw, man." Ty gave him a pitying look. "What do you think will happen when she learns the truth?"

He didn't intend to find out. Maybe there were some things that Ava would be better off not knowing.

AVA HAD ALMOST reached Davis when her phone rang. Frowning, she lifted it up, but she didn't recognize the number that appeared on her screen. "Hello?"

"He's dangerous." The words were so low she could barely understand them.

"Who is this?" Ava demanded, but...she knew.

It was him. The stalker.

"I'm just trying to protect you from him. Can't you see? I want to take care of you."

Her fingers tightened around the phone. "You almost killed Mark last night."

She heard laughter—low and bitter. "And you think Mark hasn't killed? You don't know him. Not really. He's been lying to you for so long."

"No." Ava could see Davis striding toward her. She waved to him, hoping he'd hurry forward.

"Have you asked him about the night your parents died?"

Her heart slammed against her chest. "Were you there when they died? Did you kill them?"

"Ava, I only want to take care—"

"Did you kill them?" Ava screamed.

Davis ran toward her.

"Mark is lying." His voice was still so low. "He's going to hurt you. Don't trust him."

Davis was just steps away from her.

"Ask Mark. Get him to tell you...what your father said before he died."

What?

"My father was dead when Mark got to him." She knew because Mark had told her... *I'm so sorry, Ava. There was nothing I could do. He was gone.*

"Liar, liar," that voice mocked. "You'll see soon enough. You put your trust in the wrong man."

The line went dead.

Ava stared at Davis, stricken. No, no, that creep on the phone was the one lying to her. Not Mark.

"Ava?" Davis touched her arm. "What did he say?"

"Dad was dead."

His brow furrowed.

"By the time Mark got to him, Dad was dead, wasn't he?"

Mark had said—and Davis—

Davis looked away from her.

She grabbed his shirtfront. "Dad was dead!"

"He only lived a few moments, Ava." The words were soft, sad. "He didn't have a chance of surviving."

And it felt as if she'd just been shot in the chest. "No. Mark said...you—you *both* said that he was dead. That nothing could be done!"

His fingers curled around hers. "I read the medical reports. There *was* nothing that Mark could do. Dad had lost too much blood. His wounds were too bad. But, yes..." Now his voice turned hoarse. "He was alive, just for a few minutes. Mark told me—"

"But no one told *me*!" No one but that freak on the phone. The man who was tormenting her.

"We didn't want to hurt you, Ava! That's why we held back. We didn't want you to know..." His voice trailed away into silence.

Too late. She knew exactly what he'd been about to say. "You didn't want me to know that when I left him, Dad was still alive."

Run.

Her whole body felt numb right then. "What did he say to Mark?"

Davis frowned at her.

"Before he died, what did Dad say to Mark?"

But Davis shook his head. "Nothing, Ava. Mark never told me about anything our father said to him."

Was it another lie? Or the truth? She'd trusted her brothers—and Mark—blindly for all of these years. But they'd been holding back on her.

She turned away from Davis, but he caught her shoulder. "Ava, you were so close to breaking back then…"

Everyone always thought she was so fragile.

"We were just trying to protect you."

Ava glanced at him. "I've never lied to you."

Pain flashed on his face.

"How many lies have you told me?"

He didn't answer, and that very silence terrified her.

"What else are you keeping from me? What else is Mark holding back?" Mark, the man she'd thought of as her white knight. Now he, too, seemed surrounded by secrets.

"Mark's past is his own to share." Davis swallowed. She saw the quick dip of his Adam's apple. "And anything I've done, it's all been for you."

Was that supposed to make it right?

"Let me go, Davis."

His hand lifted.

"I need some space."

"Ava…" A warning edge entered his voice.

She stiffened her spine. "Despite what you think, I'm not close to breaking apart. And I don't have a death wish. I just want to be by myself for a few hours. Is that so wrong?" She needed to get away, to stop feeling watched. "I'm going to the museum." Because she actually did have a job waiting for her. Ava's boss had called earlier and told her that they were setting up a new exhibit. More hands were needed. Kristin had said that if Ava was available to come in early, her help would be appreciated.

A couple of hours at the museum—yes, that would be just what she needed. Work, to take her mind off the insanity around her.

"If anything happens…if you need me…"

Ava looked back at him. "I need you to figure out who just called me." She tossed her phone to him. He caught it easily. "And I want to find out how he knew our father lived until Mark arrived. He said…he said that Dad spoke to Mark."

Davis stared down at her phone. "Mark never mentioned anything—"

"Yes, well, as you said, people lie." Her breath heaved out. "And I think it's long past time that we started sharing the truth."

He pulled out his phone. "Take mine. Just in case—"

"In case a crazy stalker tries to ruin my life again?" She took the phone from him. "Got it."

Then she turned and walked away. Davis didn't seem to get just how much his words had hurt her. She was tired of being in the dark. Tired of her brothers thinking she couldn't handle the danger that had haunted her family for years.

She wasn't going to break. She wasn't going to shatter into a million pieces.

No matter what happened, she'd survive.

One way or another...

Chapter Eight

"That looks amazing!" Kristin Lang said as she headed into the museum's main gallery. Her red hair was in a long braid down her back, and the large hoop earrings she wore swayed with her movements. "You've grouped them perfectly! Those colors—the lighting—fantastic!"

Ava dusted off her hands on her jeans as she glanced over at the museum's director. Kristin was only a few years older than Ava, and she seemed to be bursting with energy. A wide smile lit Kristin's face as her gaze traveled around the display.

Ava had been working with the docents there for the past three hours. They'd arranged, then rearranged the artwork until everything was perfect.

"Hiring you was the smartest move I've made in months," Kristin said, with a decisive nod.

"Uh, yes, about that..." Ava cleared her throat as she closed in on the other woman. "Why did you hire me?"

Kristin's smile slipped a notch.

And Ava's stomach knotted.

"Well, because of your credentials, of course!" Kristin told her, that smile appearing again, only it wasn't quite so full this time. "You graduated at the top of your class. You have a keen eye—" she waved her hand around the gallery "—obviously! You know your work and—"

"How much influence did the museum board have on your decision?" Because as she'd worked, she'd had time—too much time—to think about things. About the perfect job that had opened up and brought her right back home. A job that had been arranged for her... courtesy of Mark?

"The board?" Guilt sparked in Kristin's eyes. "They can make recommendations, certainly, but the final call is mine."

And Ava knew her suspicions were dead-on. "A board member told you to hire me."

"I simply went over the list of applicants, and you were personally recommended—"

"Who recommended me?" She kept her tone polite, curious, when she wanted to demand. But she couldn't demand. This was her boss, after all, and she needed the job. With everything else in her life going to hell, this position was important.

Kristin appeared hesitant.

"I have to thank him...or her," Ava said, forcing a smile of her own. One that felt incredibly stiff on her lips. "I'd hoped to get a job at a museum like this one, and that recommendation...it made my dream come true." And that was the truth.

Kristin's shoulders relaxed. "I knew you'd love this place! After our interview, I thought for certain you'd fit perfectly here! And they were both so adamant that you were the right choice—"

"Both?" Ava asked her carefully.

"Why, yes, two board members were very supportive of you. Alan Channing and Mark Montgomery. They both vouched for you, and with references like those, I wasn't about to turn you away."

Right. Ava's gaze fell to the canvas near her.

"Is everything okay?" Kristin asked as she edged closer. "You *are* enjoying the job here, aren't you?"

Ava nodded and smiled again. She hoped the smile didn't look as fake as it felt. "Of course." But…she wished Mark had told her that he'd pushed to get her the position. There were a lot of things that she wished Mark had told her.

"Wonderful." Kristin clapped excitedly. The woman really had a lot of excess energy. "And I think we're done for the day. I owe you a million thanks for coming in and helping today. You are a phenomenal addition to the museum, and I know we're going to be doing great things together."

Then Kristin was hurrying away, her high heels echoing in the museum. Ava glanced down at her watch. It was nearly five o'clock. Another night was closing in, and she still didn't have any clue who that jerk out there was.

Grant had called her twice—checking in with his usual big brother style. She'd assured him that she was fine.

I can't be afraid every moment.

Ava hurried back to her office and reached for her bag. As she'd told Grant, she couldn't let this guy control her life. She couldn't stay with a guard every moment—that was no way to live. *I won't let him win.*

Winning and losing—as if this were all some sort of sick game. Unfortunately, Ava had started to think of this whole mess as a cat-and-mouse game. She was the mouse, and the guy was just playing with her.

A few of the other workers called out to Ava as they left. She waved to them and quickly finished organizing her office. When she was satisfied, she reached for her keys. The parking garage was on the level right below the lobby, so she headed for the elevator.

"Wait for me!" Kristin called.

Ava held the elevator door for her. Kristin hurried in, carrying a big briefcase. "Late-night work," Kristin told her with a light laugh. "I've really got to learn how to leave this stuff here. Working all night doesn't give me much of a social life."

The elevator dinged when it reached the parking garage.

"Got big plans for the night?" Kristin asked her. "I know you've got family here—"

The elevator opened.

"—so I'm sure they're glad to have you back—*aah!*" Kristin's words ended in a scream because she'd just stepped out of the elevator and run right into a man wearing a black ski mask. A man armed with a knife.

He struck out with the knife, but Kristin lifted her briefcase. The blade sank into the case, and Ava grabbed Kristin, hauling her back while the man in the mask tried to yank his knife out of the leather. When Kristin was safely out of the way, Ava leapt forward. She shoved into the case, into the attacker, and he fell to the floor.

"*Ava!*"

At Kristin's cry, Ava jumped back into the elevator. Her hand slammed into the elevator's control panel. "Shut, shut, shut," she screamed. The doors started to slide closed.

The attacker was on his feet again. He had the knife in his hand.

He could have lunged forward—could have gotten in there with them.

He didn't move.

The elevator doors slid closed, and the elevator rose up to the next floor.

Kristin had a death grip on Ava's arm. "We have to call the cops!"

They had to get someplace safe first. The elevator doors were already opening. "We have to get out of this building." Ava shot out of the elevator. "Because he could be coming up the stairs." And the stairwell was just a few feet away. Was it her imagination? Or did she hear him in that stairwell right then?

They ran. They raced through the museum. Everyone else seemed to have gone, but Ava knew the security guard would still be at the front desk. They just had to get to Frank Minnow. He'd help them. He'd—

The lights flashed off.

And Ava knew that her stalker was hunting them.

"So…you've been honest with me, haven't you, Mark?"

At Davis's slow words, Mark glanced up at the guy. They were in Mark's barn, and Dr. Myers had finally gotten Legacy stable. She'd had to give the horse several injections, but he seemed calm now.

When he glanced over at Davis, Mark saw that the other man's eyes were on the pretty doctor.

"I don't like it when people lie to me," Davis continued softly.

Right. So while the guy might appear to be staring at the doc, Mark knew Davis's attention was wholly on him. "If you're going to accuse me of something, then do it." He wasn't in the mood to play games.

"You told me that my dad was still alive when you got to the ranch that night."

Mark locked his jaw. "He was." But he hadn't lived long. When he'd first seen him, Mark had thought he was already dead. There had been so much blood.

Then he'd caught the faintest sound—a whisper. He'd rushed forward and tried to stop that massive blood flow, but it had done no good.

"What did he say to you?"

Surprise pushed through Mark.

Davis turned away from the stall and focused his assessing stare fully on Mark. "Before he died, what did my father tell you?"

Mark shook his head.

"He *did* say something to you, didn't he?"

"How do you know this?" Because he hadn't thought anyone knew. Those last few moments had been so chaotic. He'd barely heard the man's rasping words.

"That psycho who is stalking Ava called her today. He told her that Dad was still alive when you got to the ranch."

Mark squeezed his eyes closed. Now he'd have to explain to Ava why he hadn't revealed that to her before. *Because I didn't want to hurt her. I didn't want Ava to know her dad was in agony until the very end. Choking on his own blood and struggling for every single breath.*

"I tried to trace the number, but it didn't work. The jerk probably was using a burner phone that he ditched right after he made the call to her."

Mark's hands were clenched into fists.

"He knew my dad was alive, and he knew that my father spoke to you before he died." Davis took a step toward Mark. His voice dropped even more as he said,

"You never told me that, man. We've spent years trying to find out who killed him, and you've been holding out on me, haven't you? You have! I can see it in your eyes."

Mark didn't speak.

Davis lunged forward. He grabbed Mark by the shirt-front. "What were you keeping from us?" Now his voice was a snarl.

Mark didn't speak.

"Stop it!" Jamie Myers yelled as she hurried toward them. "What are you two doing?" She pushed between them. Put a hand on each of their chests. "What is happening here?"

So much that the lady didn't understand.

"It didn't matter," Mark finally gritted out to Davis.

"It matters to me." Davis's breath heaved out. "What did he say to you?"

Mark looked away.

Jamie just stood there. "Please tell me that you two aren't about to start fighting. Because if that happens, someone is going to the hospital. I patch up animals, not people."

He wasn't going to fight Davis. He wouldn't do anything to hurt the guy, because then Ava would just get hurt. Wasn't that why he'd kept silent for so long? Because he didn't want to hurt her? *Everything* he did… it was all for Ava.

"Tell me," Davis demanded.

Mark raked a hand over his face. "He said…'I'm sorry.' That's all he was saying, all right? Over and over, he was trying to say he was sorry. Like it was his fault that he and his wife had been murdered."

Davis blanched.

Mark lunged forward, pushing past Jamie. He

grabbed his friend's arm. "He didn't know what was even happening then. He was out of his head. Your father wasn't to blame. No matter what—"

"He said something else." Davis's face was stark. *"Tell me."*

Jaw locking, Mark told him, "He...he said, 'My fault.' That was the last thing, okay? He was saying, 'My fault that she—'" Mark stopped because Ava's father had stopped. "He never finished that sentence."

Because he hadn't taken another breath.

Davis turned away from him.

"You were all hurt enough!" Mark yelled. "That wasn't going to help you!"

Davis kept walking.

THE MUSEUM'S ALARM was sounding. A long, desperate shriek. Kristin and Ava were running for the front doors. They rounded a corner.

"Freeze!" It was Frank, holding up his gun and flashlight.

They froze.

"Ms. McGuire? Ms. Lang?" He started to lower his weapon. "I thought everyone had already left!"

Ava shook her head. That alarm was still shrieking. "There's a man in the parking garage. He's got a knife."

Frank surged forward.

"He tried to stab me," Kristin said, her words and her body shaking. "He nearly killed me!"

Frank's light shone behind them. No one was there. But that guy in the ski mask could be *anywhere* right then.

"The police are already on the way. They were contacted the minute the alarm sounded," Frank said. "Let's get you two someplace safe."

But at this point, Ava was starting to wonder if any safe place existed.

He's always playing his games. And tonight, Kristin was almost caught in the crossfire.

They hurried down the hall. Frank stayed close, and he kept his weapon at the ready.

When they made it to the front of the museum, Ava saw the blue swirl of police lights. Frank opened the door for her and Kristin. As they rushed out, the cops rushed in. Ava glanced back—and saw all of the lights in the museum flash back on.

Cat and mouse. How long would it be until the cat decided to eat that mouse and end the game?

Kristin was talking quickly beside her. The other woman's words were tumbling out as she spoke with the uniformed cops. Ava stood there, and she just felt…cold.

I want this to end.

A car braked nearby, the squeal of its tires jarring Ava enough that she glanced to the right. She saw Alan jump out of a Jaguar. He hurried toward her. "Ava! Kristin! What's happening?" Worry darkened his face. "Was there a break-in at the museum?"

Ava shook her head. The attacker hadn't been trying to steal anything. He'd just been after her. *And he was willing to hurt Kristin because she was in his way.*

"A man tried to attack me!" Kristin said. "He was waiting in the parking garage with a knife. He—"

"It's my fault." Ava knew her voice was too low. She cleared her throat and tried again. "I'm…I'm sorry, Kristin."

Kristin's lips parted in surprise.

A young uniformed cop stepped closer. "Ma'am? You want to explain that a little bit more to me?"

She shivered. Alan took off his jacket and wrapped it around her shoulders.

"I…a man has been stalking me." Her temples were pounding. *Kristin could have died. Just like Mark could have died when the stalker went after him!* "I've already spoken with some detectives at the station. They know…he's been following me. A man in a black ski mask. A guy about six-foot-two, maybe one hundred eighty pounds."

"Ski mask," Kristin repeated, and she wrapped her arms around her stomach.

"He shot at a…friend of mine last night." Her gaze fell to the ground. "He's not stopping," she said, voice breaking a bit. "I don't think he's ever going to stop until he gets what he wants."

"And he wants…?" The cop stared at her, his eyes suspicious.

"Me."

MARK CAUGHT DAVIS right before the guy climbed into his vehicle. "Wait, man, *wait*!"

Davis looked back at him.

"Your father was a good man. We both know that. He was out of his head at the end. He was just talking crazy. I wasn't going to repeat what he said because I knew the gossips would run wild with all kinds of stories." Just like they'd done with Ava. "I didn't want your family hearing or seeing stories about your father being in on the attack…or him doing something to get your mother killed."

Davis's eyes were angry slits of green fire.

"You saw what they did to Ava!" Mark shook his head. "I was trying to protect you all. I didn't want you to hurt anymore." And they'd all been suffering through hell.

"What else aren't you telling me?"

Mark stilled.

"Because you see, Mark, I'm wondering...maybe I shouldn't be trusting you quite so much." He stepped closer. "I know what you're capable of doing. I saw you in the field. No hesitations. Anything necessary to get the job done."

Mark's back teeth had clenched. "You were the same way."

"I know." Davis eased out a breath. "That's what scares me."

Before he could speak, Mark's phone rang. He pulled it out of his pocket, then frowned at the number there. According to the name on the screen, Davis was calling him.

Only Davis was standing there, glaring at him.

Mark took the call, turning it on speaker. "Hello."

"Mark." Ava said his name in a quick rush. He could hear her fear, and every single muscle in his body locked down. "He was here, at the museum."

"Are you all right?" he immediately demanded. "Ava—"

"The alarm went off, and the police are here now. They're looking for him." Her breath whispered over the line on a soft sigh. "He had a knife."

Bastard.

"My boss, Kristin, was with me. He tried to stab her." Davis swore.

"We're both okay," Ava told them. There was no

emotion in her voice, and that scared Mark. Everything about this messed up situation scared him. "The security guard was still here. The guy after us—he turned off all the lights in the museum. He was hunting us."

But they'd gotten out. This time.

He looked up and saw the same fear and fury he felt reflected in Davis's eyes. "Stay with the cops," Mark said. "We're on our way."

HE DROVE SCARY fast to get to Ava. Mark hadn't been able to find Ty before he'd left the ranch, but Jamie had been there, still keeping watch on Legacy. He'd given orders to a few of his other ranch hands to help her— and to keep an eye on the place.

Davis was in the car with him. With every second that passed, Mark's fury grew. Why couldn't they seem to catch this guy? Why was he always a step ahead—a step that put him far too close to Ava?

When he got to the museum, he counted five police cars at the scene. The area looked like chaos, with the uniformed cops all running around. He knew the system must have automatically sent an alert to the authorities when the museum's alarm had triggered.

I hope you left a trail behind this time.

He jumped from his vehicle and hurried toward the building. Then he saw Ava. She was standing to the side, talking with two cops. Alan Channing was with her. As Mark watched, Alan wrapped his arm around Ava and gave her a hug.

Mark hurried toward them.

"I'll take Ava home," Alan was saying. "Until this bastard is caught, I feel like she needs someone to stay close to her."

Ava rubbed her left temple. "I don't want anyone else getting pulled into this mess. I'm fine on my own."

But Alan shook his head. "You need—"

"Ava." Mark slid past the police officers.

Alan stiffened. His arm dropped from Ava's shoulders.

Mark reached out to her. His hand skimmed down her cheek even as his eyes searched every inch of her for any sign of injury. "Did he hurt you?"

"No. He—he almost stabbed Kristin." She pointed to the right. The redhead was talking animatedly with more cops. "The knife went into her briefcase instead of slicing into her, and I shoved him back."

Davis pushed Mark to the side. Mark glared at the guy.

"The elevator closed, and we got away from him." Her gaze drifted to the museum. "Then the lights went out."

"Where were you when the guy attacked?" Davis asked.

"The parking garage. We were leaving. The doors opened, and he was just there."

Because he'd been waiting on her.

"The others had just left a few moments before. There's so much security at the museum, I-I thought I was safe."

He'd thought she was safe there, too. So when Davis had told him earlier that Ava had gone in to work a few hours at the museum, he'd figured she was getting some much needed downtime.

"When he cut the lights, he might have thought that also disconnected the security system," Davis muttered.

"It didn't. The alarm was shrieking so loudly, I thought my eardrums were about to burst."

Maybe that alarm had scared the guy away.

Davis hugged her. Ava seemed stiff in his arms. And actually, Mark realized that when he'd touched her cheek earlier, Ava hadn't moved at all.

"I was about to take Ava home," Alan said. "That is...if you're done talking with her?" he asked the cops.

They nodded.

"I can take my sister home," Davis said, voice tight. "But thanks, Channing."

"Actually, I can take myself home," Ava said with a tired smile. "But thank you, Alan. I mean it. I appreciate the offer."

Alan hesitated. His gaze seemed to soften as it slid over Ava's face. "I wouldn't ever want anything to happen to you."

Ava shrugged out of the coat she'd been wearing and gave it back to Alan. "Thank you."

And the guy still lingered.

Ava hadn't looked at Mark, not directly in the eyes, since he'd arrived. He'd been expecting something else. What, exactly, he didn't know. But Ava just seemed cold, and that wasn't her. Ava was passion and heat and emotion—not this.

"Kristin is shaken," Ava said, her gaze troubled. "We need to make sure that she gets home all right."

"We can take her," Davis immediately began.

But Alan told them, "I've got her. Don't worry. I'll see to it that Kristin gets home safely." He inclined his head toward them, letting his stare stay on Ava a bit too long. Then he turned and made his way toward Kristin.

Davis pressed even closer to Ava. "Were you able to tell anything else about the guy this time?"

"He was still wearing a ski mask."

Mark wanted to pull her into his arms and hold her tight. But she was actually inching away from him.

"The garage was well lit, right?" Davis pressed her. "Did you see his eyes?"

Ava pushed back her hair. "It all happened so fast. The doors opened, and he was just there with that knife. Kristin lifted her briefcase, and the knife came down." She licked her lips. "I pulled her back and shoved him down. I don't think…" Her head tilted as she seemed to remember the scene. "I don't think I ever saw his eyes. I don't remember them, anyway. So fast…" Her words trailed away.

"I want to talk with Kristin," Davis said. "See if she can remember anything else about the guy." He hurried toward the redhead.

Mark stayed right there. Ava still wasn't looking at him. Was it because of what that jerk had told her on the phone call?

"I've had enough," Ava said.

His heart stopped right then.

"I'm not going to let him hurt anyone else just because he's after me." She whirled away from Mark and stared out in the darkness. "He's out there right now, watching me."

"Ava…"

"First you, then Kristin. Who will be next? Who is he going to hurt because he wants to get to me?" Her voice was getting louder, sharper. A few of the cops glanced their way. "No one else," she said. Her words seemed to ring in the night. "You want me? Then just come for me. *Leave everyone else alone!*"

Silence.

Ava's breath heaved out.

Mark wrapped his arms around her. He hated her pain. If he could, he'd take it all way.

"LEAVE EVERYONE ELSE ALONE."
He almost smiled when Ava shouted those words. Finally she understood. This was just about the two of them. The way it should always have been.

As he watched, she jerked away from Mark. She was realizing that Mark and his lies were no good for her.

Ava didn't have blinders on any longer. She wasn't hiding. She was ready to face all of the dark truths out there.

She was asking for him. Calling out to him because…
Ava is ready for me now.
He was certainly ready for her.

Chapter Nine

"Ava." Mark held her tight, his mouth close to her ear as he said, "Baby, you're tearing me apart."

As always, his touch seemed to warm her, but her pain was strong right then. She was tired of others being at risk for her. The next time that stalker attacked, he could wind up killing someone.

She pulled away from Mark. A fast glance to the right showed her that Davis was with Kristin. No doubt grilling her. So much for the fresh start at a new job. When you nearly got your boss killed, that made one heck of an impression.

"Let's go back to the cottage," Mark told her.

Back to hide again.

She looked around once more. He was out there. She knew it. Would he follow her back to the ranch? *I want this to end.*

"Ava!" Davis called her name, and she looked up to see him jogging toward her.

"I'm going home," she said. Because she needed to think. Just standing out there with those swirling blue lights was giving her a headache.

Davis looked at Mark. She sighed. "I have my own car. I can get home just fine—"

"I'm sure that's what Mark thought last night," Davis drawled, "until the guy opened fire on him."

Ava flinched.

"For me, please let Mark take you home."

Her lips thinned.

"I want to stay and talk to the cops, and I kind of need your car so that I can get back home." He rolled his shoulders back. "When Mark and I realized what was happening, we both just jumped into one of the cars he keeps at his ranch."

She fished for her keys and held them out to Davis. "Be careful."

His fingers closed around the keys. "Always."

Ava headed toward Mark's car. A quick glance over her shoulder showed Ava that Davis was already closing in on Kristin Lang and the cops near her.

"Maybe the guy who did this left evidence behind this time," Mark said.

Or maybe he'd gotten away clean again.

Ava slid into the car. Mark didn't shut her door. He knelt down so that they were eye to eye. The open car door was behind him, partially shielding his body. "I know that he called you."

More pain. She was so tired of the pain. "You lied to me."

"I was—"

"Please, don't say you were protecting me," Ava told him as she rubbed her throbbing right temple. "Right now that's the last thing I want to hear."

His gaze held hers. He gave a grim nod and rose.

She caught his hand. "What did my father say to you?"

He looked away. *Another secret.* They sure were

piling up. "What did my father say?" Ava asked again. "And how did *he* know?"

"Your father said that he was sorry."

His words squeezed her heart.

"And that it was his fault."

Ava started to shake her head.

"That's what your father said. It was his fault. Those were his last words to me, Ava, I swear it." The faint lines near his mouth deepened. "There was no point in telling you what he'd said back then. The last thing I wanted to do was hurt you any more. You were in enough pain. As it was, Davis and I were already afraid—" He broke off and looked away. As if he couldn't quite bear to look her in the eye.

But Ava knew what he'd been going to say. "You thought I was going to hurt myself, didn't you?"

He nodded.

"I didn't want to die back then, Mark. Not then, not now." She pulled her seat belt into place. He slammed the car door and hurried around to the driver's side.

Mark started to crank up the car, but she stopped him. Her fingers curled around his wrist. "You still didn't tell me… How does my stalker know what my dad said?"

"I don't know. I didn't think *anyone* had heard him speaking to me. I was there with Ty and a few other ranch hands, but they weren't close, not during those final moments."

Ty? "Where is he now?" Ava asked softly. "Where's Ty?"

Mark turned to stare at her. "He wasn't at the ranch when I left. So I don't—*you think it's Ty?*"

"I think the man who called me on the phone…he

was disguising his voice. Probably because he was afraid I'd recognize it—him—if he didn't. I think he's around Ty's height and build, and I think Ty is one of the few people who knew that my father spoke to you before he died." She pulled in a deep breath. "And right now, the thing I want most...is to find Ty."

He cranked the car. "Then let's hunt him down."

"I DIDN'T SEE his eyes. I'm sorry," Kristin Lang said as she swiped her hand over her cheek. "I just saw the knife coming right at me."

Davis had sure hoped that Kristin would remember more about the attacker.

"He was waiting down there." Her voice was hollow. "Other people had gone into the parking garage before us, but he must have been hiding. *Waiting*," she said once more.

For Ava.

"Is he going to come after me again?" Kristin asked him, her eyes wide with fear and her lips trembling. "Ava said that he's been stalking her. Do you think he'll come back to the museum?"

Davis thought the man had to be stopped—yesterday.

"Let me take you home, Kristin," Alan said. He put his hand on her shoulder.

She turned toward him, nodding. "Th-thank you."

Davis watched them leave. Something was nagging at him. "Kristin!"

She looked back at him.

"He struck out with his knife once, right?"

Biting her lip, she nodded.

"He didn't try to attack again?"

"Ava pushed him down. He had to yank the knife out

of the briefcase. By the time he got back up, the elevator doors were starting to close." She shuddered. "I've never been so afraid in my entire life."

Alan led her away. His Jaguar waited near the corner.

Davis turned and strode into the museum. Most of the cops there knew him, so they let him into what normally would've been a closed crime scene. In moments, he was down in the parking garage, searching the scene. There were no video cameras down there. No wonder the guy had been lying in wait in that particular spot. Instead of going into the museum, it would have been much easier just to sit back and have his prey come to him.

Davis paced a few feet away from the elevator. A large column stretched to the ceiling. It would have been easy enough to hide near the column and still have a perfect view of that elevator.

You thought Ava would come down alone, didn't you? But she wasn't alone, so you had to try and get Kristin out of your way.

He edged around the column. The stairs were to the right. It would have been easy enough for the man to rush up there...

Davis pushed open the door. It groaned. The stairwell was dark. He took his time going up those stairs, searching carefully. Then he was at the first floor. He eased into the hallway. And saw the first sensor near an exhibit on his left.

You set off the sensor. You never intended to come this far, but you couldn't let Ava get away, could you?

And when the alarms had started shrieking, the man would have gone for the fastest exit—and that would have been the stairwell again. He would have gone out that way.

Davis headed back downstairs. Only a few cars were left in the garage.

Did you just drive away while the alarms were shrieking?

He walked out of the garage, heading for the main street. He took the same path that a vehicle would have needed to take. And it was there, about ten feet from the garage's exit, that he found the discarded ski mask. It had been tossed into a garbage can, one the city had placed right at the edge of the road.

Davis stared at that mask. "Got you." Because he was sure the man he was after had left trace evidence in that mask. Maybe something as small as a hair, but it would be *something*.

He looked up and realized that…Alan Channing had been parked right at that same spot. His Jaguar had been there moments before.

And now he was gone…with Kristin Lang.

WHEN MARK PULLED up at his ranch, the place looked quiet. Too quiet. The doors to the stables were shut. No one was out patrolling. The lights in the main house were all turned off.

"Where is everyone?" Ava asked.

He killed the engine and climbed from the car. "Let's find out."

Ava hurriedly exited the vehicle and followed him. He went to the stables first and pushed open the doors. He braced himself before he entered, more than half-afraid that he'd discover his horses had been attacked again.

But when he entered the stables, Jamie was still

there. She turned and saw him and Ava, and the doc smiled. "He's doing great." She stood next to Legacy and patted the horse. "Give him a day and he should be as good as new."

His breath expelled in a rush. "Thank you."

She inclined her head toward him. "I'm just glad I could help." She made her way out of the stall. "But you should know…it was close, Mark. Someone didn't just want to hurt that animal. Someone deliberately poisoned him with a very high dose of drugs. That person wanted Legacy to die."

Because that SOB was trying to hurt me.

She made her way past Mark and Ava. "Hopefully you won't need me again." She reached for the door. "But if you do, you know where I am." The door squeaked when she left.

Mark stared at Legacy. The horse walked toward him, and Mark reached out to stroke Legacy between his eyes.

"I'm sorry," Ava said as she edged closer to him. "This should never have happened."

No, it shouldn't have happened.

Jaw locking, Mark turned around. He had quarters for his ranch hands out back. And if the men weren't patrolling, then he should be able to find them there. His steps were fast, angry, as he went straight to that area. Ava rushed to keep up with him.

The main ranch house had been dark, but the quarters for the men—they were lit up. He could hear the sound of voices and laughter drifting in the air. When he got to the door, he pounded his fist against the surface.

The door was opened quickly, and one of the youngest hands on the ranch, Pape Forrest, stood there. The guy, barely nineteen, swiped his hair back and straightened when he saw that Mark was the person who'd been pounding on his door. "Boss? Did you come to join the game?"

Mark looked over Pape's shoulder. The workers were gathered around a table—poker night. Right. He'd forgotten all about that. Sometimes he joined in the games. They were a great way to let off steam after a hellish week.

But he wasn't there to play. "I need to speak with Ty."

Ty stood. A line of chips was spread out in front of him. "What's up?"

Ava was silent behind Mark. "Let's go outside," he told his friend. Outside and away from the eyes and ears of the other men there.

Ty took his time heading toward Mark. He pulled the door shut behind him. The sun was setting, the sky darkening, and shadows were snaking across the ranch.

Ty looked at first Mark, then Ava. He exhaled heavily. "Why do I feel like I won't enjoy this little talk?"

He is my friend. He'd been close to Ty for years. The man knew all his secrets. "Where were you earlier?"

Ty frowned at the question. "I went to visit my girl, Mary, at her apartment. She'd made a late lunch for me."

Mary. Right. That would be Mary Angel. A sweet blonde who Ty had dated on and off for a few years. Mark had thought that Ty and Mary were currently off, but maybe they were an item again.

"What's going on?"

Ava stepped forward. "You were there the night my father died."

"Yes." Sadness whispered in his voice. "And that's a sight I won't ever be forgetting."

"You knew my father was alive when Mark got to him."

Ty's stare jerked to Mark. "You told her?"

"No, the man who has been stalking her did that." He kept his voice emotionless. "He called Ava and told her about her father's last minutes and about her dad's final words."

Ty took a step back. "He *spoke* to you, Mark? I-I didn't know. He was breathing, but it was a bare thing. I can't believe—*he spoke to you*?"

His shock seemed real.

"I didn't know." Ty shook his head. "I mean, I knew he was hanging on, barely, but the guy was bleeding all over the place. I almost fell in the blood that covered the floor—"

Ava gave a choked cry.

"I'm sorry!" Ty said at once. He yanked a hand through his hair. "You didn't need to hear that. You didn't need…" His words trailed away. His head cocked as he studied Mark. "Why are you asking me these questions? About where I was? About what I *might* have heard all those years ago?"

Mark braced his legs apart. "Ava's stalker made an appearance earlier. He came to the art museum, armed with a knife…and isn't Mary's place just a few blocks from that art museum?"

Ty's mouth dropped open as he seemed to understand Mark's questions—and his suspicions. *"You think I went after your girl?"*

At this point, Mark didn't know what to think.

"No, *no*." The denial was sharp. "Call Mary. She'll

back me up. I didn't do that. Come on, you *know* me, man. I would never do anything to hurt a woman. Not after the hell I saw my own mother endure."

Because she'd been a victim, too. Ty had never mentioned specifics to Mark, but he'd let just enough slip over the years that Mark had realized Ty's mother had been abused by a lover. To escape from that pain, she'd turned to booze. *It numbs everything for her.* Ty had told him that long ago.

"I've always had your back," Ty told him, voice roughening. "Even when old man Montgomery passed—right after you—" He stopped, his chin jutting up in the air. "I never said a thing to the cops, did I?"

Mark's drumming heartbeat filled his ears. He was aware of Ava stiffening. "There was nothing to tell the cops," Mark said flatly.

"You threatened to kill him, man. Said he should pay for all the pain he'd caused. I heard you tell him that you knew what he'd done to the McGuires…" Ty cast an apologetic look at Ava. "And the next day, he was dead."

"Mark?" Ava's voice was stunned.

"I didn't say anything to the cops," Ty continued quickly. "Because I have your back. Always. So if you think I would ever do anything to hurt your girl, you are dead wrong."

ALAN CHANNING LIVED in a high-rise condo in downtown Austin. Davis rode the elevator up to the guy's floor, his body tight with tension. He'd turned over that ski mask to the cops, but even before the crime scene techs had collected the important evidence, he'd seen the hairs stuck in the material.

Blond hairs.

The elevator opened, and Davis stalked down the hallway. The thick carpet muffled the sound of his footsteps. In moments he was in front of Alan's door. Jaw locking, Davis lifted his hand and knocked.

Silence.

He waited, his impatience growing by the moment. He'd called Grant on the way over, and his brother was already digging into Alan Channing's past. The guy had been at the scene tonight—too conveniently so—and if those blond hairs were linked to him...

You will go down for hurting my sister.

The door creaked open. Alan's eyes flared in surprise when he saw Davis.

"Wh-what are you doing here?" Alan asked him. "Is Ava all right?"

Ava. "Mind if I come in?" Davis asked.

Alan blinked. "Uh, of course, come on in." He stepped back. "I just got in myself. I had to stay with Kristin for a little while. She was quite flustered after the attack tonight."

Davis thought "flustered" was quite an understatement. His gaze darted around the condo. The guy had obviously used an interior designer on the place. It looked like something out of a magazine—something perfect but untouched. There were no personal pictures in the place. No mementos. Just cold class.

"Ava is okay, isn't she?"

Wanting to gauge his reaction, Davis turned his full attention back on the other man. "She left with Mark. I'm sure he's keeping a very close eye on her."

Alan's lips tightened. "I thought you were taking her home."

"Ava wanted Mark."

Ah, there it was. A flash of anger on the guy's face. "Ava could do far better than Mark Montgomery."

He eased closer to the man. "Why were you at the museum tonight?"

Alan stepped back. "I'm on the board. I often go the museum—"

"But it wasn't open to the public today." He knew. He'd done plenty of checking. "They were working on a new exhibit. It was staff only."

"I'm on the board!" Alan said again. "I was appointed recently, and I like to check up on things—"

"You've been making a lot of trips over to Houston in the last few months." That was a total shot in the dark. Yes, Grant was checking for trips like that right then—but they didn't know anything about the guy so far. All Davis had was his growing suspicion.

But at his words, Alan's lips parted in surprise, and his head jerked. "That's business! Just business!"

Well, well...

"My business takes me all over Texas. And yes, I have to visit Houston frequently. What does that matter?"

It mattered a great deal because... "Ava was living in Houston."

Alan nodded. "Right, but Ava hadn't seen me in ages. We ran into one another recently at the museum, we talked about grabbing a bite to eat together—and that is all." The guy was sweating.

"Interesting phrasing you have there... Ava hadn't seen *you*. But had you seen Ava?"

Alan's chin hitched up. "I worried about her. She had a hard time after her parents died."

Davis's body tensed. "You don't have to tell me that. She's my sister. I know all about her."

"No," Alan said softly. "I don't think you do. You still see her as that lost sixteen-year-old, but she isn't that girl any longer." Like he needed this guy telling him anything about Ava.

"Ava is so much more than you realize," Alan continued, voice almost passionate. "I've always known that about her."

The guy was talking about Ava as if he were still in love with her. And when Davis had seen them at the museum, Alan's face had flashed with jealousy when Mark got near her.

Alan straightened his shoulders. "I don't understand why you're here."

"I'm here because some psycho has been terrorizing my sister, and I don't like for Ava to be afraid."

"I don't, either," Alan said at once.

Davis smiled at him. He knew it wasn't a pretty sight. "You don't want me for an enemy."

Alan's cheeks flushed red as he sucked in a sharp breath. "Are you threatening me?"

"No, I'm stating a fact. You don't want me for an enemy, and you don't want Mark Montgomery for an enemy."

"I'm not afraid of Montgomery!"

You should be.

"Why was Ava at the museum tonight?"

Alan's hands flew up in the air. "This is ridiculous! Obviously the woman was working. Kristin had a big project, and she needed all hands on deck."

"And you knew all about that project?"

"I told you—"

"Right, you're on the board." This guy was pushing all of Davis's buttons. "But Ava wasn't scheduled to start at the museum for a few more days. Why would Kristin call her in early?"

Alan glanced away.

"I think I'll call Kristin and find out," Davis murmured.

Alan ran a shaking hand through his hair. "I told Kristin to call Ava in."

I thought as much. You wanted Ava out in the open, didn't you? Where you could get to her?

"I knew how qualified Ava was. This—this would have been a great opportunity for her—"

"Or for you."

Alan inched back another step. "I don't know what you mean."

"It was a chance for you to get to Ava." His hands clenched into fists. "I found the ski mask you left behind."

"What ski mask?"

"The one you were wearing when you tried to stab Kristin. Only she wasn't the target, right? It was Ava. You were waiting in that parking garage for her, but when the elevator opened, Ava wasn't alone. Kristin was with her. You had to get rid of Kristin, so you attacked."

"No!" Alan shook his head. "I wasn't in any parking garage! I was outside. I was coming by to see— to see if Ava wanted to have dinner with me. I didn't attack anyone."

"I found the ski mask," Davis said again. "Your hair is in it."

"My...my hair?"

"You left evidence behind. Very sloppy. But I guess

you just couldn't stand it anymore, could you? Seeing how close Ava was getting to Mark. She was supposed to come back for you, right? Not him?"

"Get out," Alan spat.

"Just how long have you been obsessed with my sister?" Davis demanded as the rage heated in his gut. "Because now I'm wondering...did it start all of those years ago? She broke up with you, right? On the same night that our parents were killed."

Alan marched to the door. He yanked it open. "Anything else you have to say to me...you can say through my attorney."

"Don't worry," Davis took his time strolling toward the door. "I'm sure the cops will have plenty to say to you *and* your attorney real soon."

Alan's body seemed to be practically vibrating with rage.

Davis stopped right next to the man. "Stay away from my sister."

Alan's eyes burned with fury. "I'm not scared of Mark Montgomery, and I'm not scared of you, either. You think because you were some hotshot SEAL that I'm supposed to tremble when you're near?"

The guy *was* trembling.

"I would never hurt Ava. Everything I've done has been to help her." He gave a rough laugh. "So do your worst. Rip into my life. Go digging for all my secrets. You'll see I'm not the one you're after."

"You'd better not be," Davis told him. "Because if you are, I will make your life a living hell."

Then he strolled out of the condo.

Alan slammed the door shut behind him.

Davis took out his phone and called Grant. "Hey,

man, you need to get that info on Alan Channing yesterday." He glanced back at the door. He knew that Brodie and Jennifer were at McGuire Securities with Grant—they were all working to dig up information on Alan Channing right then. "Because I think we may just have found Ava's stalker."

Chapter Ten

They were back at the guest cottage on the McGuire ranch. Mark turned off the car's engine, but he didn't make a move to leave the vehicle. Ava was beside him. She'd been pretty silent ever since Ty had dropped his bombshells.

He looked over at Ava. She sat there, as still as a stone. He told her, "I didn't kill him."

Ava flinched. She fumbled, opened her door and hurried from the vehicle. He followed right behind her and caught her before she could go inside the cottage. "Ava, please, wait!" He turned her around in his arms. "Listen to me, okay?"

She stared up at him. The porch light shone down on her.

"There were plenty of times when I wanted Gregory dead," Mark confessed. *More times than I can count.* "When he hurt me, when he raged and drank... I wanted him to die." The words were brutal and true. "I stayed here for my mother." She'd been sick those last few years, battling heart disease, and she'd had no idea what Gregory had done to Mark. "When she passed, I didn't plan to come back, ever."

He'd tried to hide this part of his life from Ava

because he'd been afraid she would turn away. Now he was desperate to do anything, to say anything, if he could just convince her to stay with him.

"Where did you go?" Ava asked him.

He half smiled. "Maybe I was more like your brothers than I realized back then. I joined the army. Served a tour and then I...went independent."

Most folks didn't call the contractors "mercenaries" any longer. He'd worked on jobs in so many different parts of the world. He'd seen things that he'd never be able to forget. And he'd realized...a man can only run so far from the ghosts that chased him.

"I got word that Gregory was bad. Drinking, going days without eating. He'd gotten a diagnosis of cancer, and it had driven him over the edge."

She inhaled sharply. "I didn't know—"

"No one did but me. His lawyers called me. Told me what was happening. He couldn't take care of the ranch any longer, and if I didn't come back, he was afraid he'd lose the business." Only when he'd come back, he'd learned that Gregory was still interested destroying everyone around him. "I wanted him to get clean and look for treatment options. But he told me to screw off. Said he didn't need me and never would."

"What had he done to my family?"

His hand dropped back to his side. "Your father had been plagued by poor supply shipments and overzealous creditors for years. Did you know that?"

She shook her head.

"Yeah, I didn't, either. Not until I came back. By then, Gregory wasn't able to hide his secrets from me. I found records of all the times he'd tried to cause havoc in your father's life."

Ava's eyes were so wide and deep.

"He thought he loved her," Mark said. "In his twisted way. Though I doubt he could actually love anyone. And he wanted to punish your father for taking her away."

"My mother?"

Mark nodded.

"That night—the last night he was alive—I'd found all the paperwork that showed what he'd done over the years. And even with your parents gone…" This was so hard to say to her. Especially when she was staring up at him with trust in her eyes. "I learned he was still trying to cause trouble. He should have been fighting the cancer! But he was scheming like mad and trying to get a team to come in and buy the ranch out from under your brothers."

She stepped back.

"I told him it wasn't happening. And, yeah, I said I should kill him myself. But that was just anger talking. Rage." Fury at a man who'd abused him for years— and who'd enjoyed hurting so many people. "I told him that he was a disgrace and that maybe he was better off dead. Then I left him." Guilt rose then, knifing through him. There'd been no love lost between him and Gregory but… *I would wish that death he'd suffered on no one.*

"Mark?"

"When I came back the next morning, he'd shot himself in the head."

"I'm sorry."

Her kind reaction shocked him. He had to touch her then. Had to wrap his arms around her shoulders and step even closer to her. "I told you what he did to your family."

"He was the only father you knew."

"He was a sick bastard who left me with more scars that I can count, and he harassed your family for years. No one should mourn him. No one should—"

"I'm sorry," she said again. Her voice and her touch were so very gentle. "Because I know it hurt you. No matter what he'd done, I know it hurt."

And it had. He put his forehead against hers.

Ava's hand rose and caressed his jaw. "I know you," she continued. "Even if you think you're keeping your secrets from me, I know who you are inside."

"I didn't kill him." Those words came out so gruff.

"I know."

He'd seen suspicion on so many faces—even Ty's. *Ty thinks I did it. So do others at the ranch.* But he hadn't pulled that trigger. He hadn't fired since his days in the Middle East.

Yet...

I would kill in an instant if it meant protecting her. That understanding went straight to his soul. He would truly do anything for Ava.

He pressed his lips to hers. When Ava was close, Mark felt better. Stronger. She made him want to be better. A man who was worthy of her.

The kiss deepened as he pushed her against the door.

Her taste made him heady. Desire surged through him. He couldn't be near Ava and not want her. She'd gotten beneath his skin, and he knew that he'd never be able to escape the pull she had on him.

"Come inside with me," Ava told him.

Like he needed to be asked twice.

Ava opened the door. Mark followed her inside. The

cottage was dark as he reset the locks. Ava didn't linger
in the little den. She walked straight for the bedroom.

He hesitated.

"Don't be shy now," she told him, her voice light,
soft, and banishing the grief and rage that had clung to
him for a moment. "I'm waiting on you."

"I don't have a shy bone in my body."

She slipped into the bedroom. He followed right behind her. The room smelled of Ava. Sweet strawberries.
He turned on the light because he wanted to see every
inch of her body.

She stood next to the bed and stripped. There was
no shyness from her, either. Her clothing hit the floor
with a soft rustle and she stood before him, her body
bare and perfect. Her breasts thrust toward him. The
pink tips were tight, and he wanted to taste them. Her
waist curved into the flare of her hips. Just staring at
her pretty much made him ache.

He stepped forward.

"You still have your clothes on," Ava pointed out.

Mostly because he couldn't wait to touch her. His
hand curled around her breast, then stroked that tight
nipple. Ava gave the little moan that he loved—Mark
was sure he'd already grown addicted to that sound.

He lifted her up against him, holding her easily, and
he took her nipple into his mouth. Her fingers sank into
his hair as she arched toward him. He kissed that sweet
flesh. Licked. Sucked. His mouth pressed to her as he
carried her to the bed.

He put her down on the mattress, and for a moment
he just stared at her. Lost. "You're supposed to be afraid
of me."

She reached up and slid her hand under his shirt. "I'm shaking with fear."

No, she wasn't. "When I was in the army, and after... it wasn't an easy time, baby. I did things—"

"Your mission."

Yes, but some of those missions had been horrible. Blood and death and sand and battles without end.

"I don't think I've ever been afraid of you." Now her hand was at the snap of his jeans. "And I don't think I ever could be." She unzipped his fly.

His erection sprang into her hands, and when she stroked him from root to tip, his eyes nearly rolled back in his head. Earlier he'd remembered to put another condom in his wallet—very lucky because he wasn't sure anything could have stopped him from being with her tonight.

She kept stroking him, and a growl slipped from his throat. He leaned over the bed, over her, and he braced his hands on the mattress. Mark kissed her, a caress of his lips against hers as he explored her mouth and put a stranglehold on his desire.

But Ava pulled back. "You don't have to go slow with me. I want you. I want you to make me forget everything else."

He ditched his clothes, put on the condom and went straight to her. But...

"Why do you want to be with me?" The question was pulled from him even as he caressed the slick folds of her sex. He wanted Ava so badly he hurt, but did she just want the oblivion that pleasure could give to her? Would anyone work for her right then? Would—

"Don't you know?" Her eyes held his. "Because I love you."

Time seemed to stop. He stared at her a moment, and he even shook his head, certain that he must have misheard.

But Ava smiled up at him. Her dimples flashed. "I've loved you for a long time."

She broke him.

He drove into her, thrusting deep and hard. His control had shattered as his need for her erupted. There was no holding back. No taking things slow or careful. There was only need. Only desire. Only him trying to take everything that he could—even as he gave Ava all that he had.

The bed was squeaking and slamming into the wall. Ava was gasping. Her nails dug into his back. He kissed her neck. Let her feel the score of his teeth. He wanted to mark her right then, to show others that Ava was his—because he was hers.

He didn't have the words to give her. He wasn't even sure what he should say, and all he could do right then was feel. Feel the hot heaven of her body and her silken skin.

Taste…

Taste Ava. Her lips. Lush and full, red and wet.

Take.

Take her until she screamed for him. He could feel the way her sex was squeezing around him. Ava was close to her release. So close.

"Mark!" She slammed her hips up against him, and her inner muscles clenched tightly around him.

He came, following her on that hot and heavy tide of release. He emptied into her until he was sure he had nothing left. His heart thudded. Sweat slicked his skin. And he didn't let her go.

I love you.

He knew that he'd *never* let her go again. Ava belonged with him, and now both of their fates were sealed.

DAVIS'S FOOTSTEPS WERE slow as he walked through the ranch house. The place was so quiet. Brodie and Jennifer had opted to stay in the city—they were planning to head out at first light so that they could go to Houston and learn more about Alan Channing's visits to that city.

And to see if he was watching Ava during those trips.

Exhaustion clawed at him. He'd gone back to the police station. Told the cops all he knew about Alan. The cops had promised to keep uniforms near Alan's place just as a precaution.

So you'll see what if feels like to be watched.

Mark was with Ava. They were settled in at the guest house. He'd called earlier and woken Ava from her sleep. Her voice had been husky when she told him that she was safe. That Mark was close.

He knew that Mark would die before he'd let anything happen to Ava.

I've known how the guy felt about her for years. But he'd still tried to keep Mark away from Ava. Why?

He walked through the quiet halls of the house.

Because I didn't want to lose Ava.

He climbed into bed and stared up at the ceiling. Family was the thing that mattered most to him. He knew many people thought he was a cold-blooded bastard, but his family...his family was his life.

He'd already lost so much in the past.

Too much.

The house here—this sweet spot in Texas—it was his haven. It was—

Davis smelled smoke. He could hear…the faint hiss and crackle of flames.

Fire! He lurched up and leapt for the door.

SHE'D DONE IT. Ava turned in the bed, and her gaze slid over Mark's features. She'd actually told him that she loved him.

And Mark hadn't said anything back to her.

Talk about awkward—and painful.

The sex had been incredible. They had combustible chemistry. There was no denying that. But for her, it was more than just physical, and it was far more than just sex.

I've loved him for years.

She still had no clue how Mark felt about her.

She'd slept for just a little bit and had woken to find him still in the bed next to her. His arm was curled around her stomach. He looked so…relaxed right then. Peaceful, even. She hadn't seen him look peaceful very many times in his life.

Moving so very carefully, Ava eased from beneath his arm. She grabbed a T-shirt—his—and slid it over her head. Then she tiptoed out of the room. Ava didn't take a full breath until the bedroom door shut behind her.

The little cottage was so quiet. Ava glanced around as her eyes adjusted to the darkness in the den. The porch light was spilling through the front window. She stared out that window for a moment.

When will it end?

She turned away and headed toward the back room

in the cottage. The room that housed her paintings. She opened the door. She'd poured her rage and pain into those canvases. Then she'd tried to hide them— the same way she'd tried to hide her feelings ever since she was sixteen.

But Ava was done hiding.

She flipped on the light. Then her breath choked out in a sharp cry of shock and dismay.

The canvases—they'd been slashed.

At first Ava could only shake her head. No, no, that wasn't possible. Her brothers had installed the *best* security at the ranch. No one could get inside…

But someone had. The canvases littered the floor. It looked as if someone had taken a knife to them, and she remembered the knife that had swung out at Kristin in that elevator.

Ava backed away, moving slowly out of that room, but then she bumped into something—someone—and she whirled around, screaming.

Chapter Eleven

"Ava!" Mark caught her hands when they swung out to attack him. "Baby, what's wrong—" But then he broke off because he'd just caught sight of those canvases.

"He's here." In contrast to her scream, now Ava's voice was a low whisper. "He got past the security, and he's here on the ranch."

Mark swore and pulled her from the room. No one should have been able to get on the ranch. The McGuires were fanatical about the security out there. "We need to get dressed," he told her, "and get out of here." He wanted her safe, and then he wanted to hurt this guy. Because if he was still close by...

Then I will find you.

They hurried back to Ava's bedroom and dressed as fast as they could, and then—

The lights went off.

He heard Ava suck in a sharp breath. "That's the same way it was at the museum. He killed the lights there—*he's playing with me.*"

Mark reached for his phone and called Davis. The line rang and rang—no answer.

"Mark?" Ava's fingers curled around his wrist. "Are my brothers okay?"

He put the phone in his pocket. In the dark, she couldn't see his expression, so she wouldn't know the worry that pierced through him. "Of course," he told her, forcing his voice to sound calm. "You know them— no one can take down the McGuire boys."

Get her out of here. Get her to safety.

He didn't have a weapon in the cottage, but he had one waiting in the car outside. They headed for the door, moving slowly, carefully. Mark opened the door.

And found himself staring down the barrel of a gun.

The moon was overhead, its light spilling down, so it was easy for Mark to see the weapon pointed right at him. And the man there—

"Ava," the guy demanded, his voice gruff. "What is happening?"

The man holding the gun wasn't an enemy. Mark recognized his voice even if most of the guy's body was in shadows.

Ava pushed past Mark and ran to the guy, giving him a tight hug. "Mac," she whispered.

No one can take down the McGuire boys.

And another McGuire was standing right there, holding Ava with one arm while his other hand still gripped that gun. Mac McGuire was probably the wildest—and, if the stories were true, deadliest—of the bunch. Former Delta Force, Mac seemed to enjoy looking for danger. An adrenaline junkie, some had said. Mark had always thought Mac rushed after the danger because he was running from his own demons.

"I didn't think you were in town," Ava said. "Davis told me that you were working a case in Atlanta."

"Sully and I just finished up there," Mac said, his voice gruff.

Sully—yeah, that would be the youngest McGuire. Sullivan. Ex-marine. Icy green eyes, dangerous temper.

"We came down here as soon as we could," Mac replied. He was still holding tight to the gun—and Ava. "When the lights went off, he went to the main house to check in, and I came here." He hesitated. "Ava, what is happening?"

"We all need to get up to the main house," Mark said. "The jerk who has been stalking Ava has been here."

"Then why are we just standing out in the open?" Mac demanded.

Good freaking question.

They hurried out to the cars. Mark's gaze narrowed when he looked at his tires. "Someone slashed them." *He was here...while I was in that cottage with Ava.* And Mark had been so lost in her that he hadn't even been aware of the danger.

"Is the cottage clear?" Mac's gaze had turned back to the house.

"I don't know." Mark slid closer to Ava. "I just wanted to get her out of there and..." His breath came out in a rush. "Davis wasn't answering his phone. I wanted to make sure he was safe up at the main house." That they'd all been safe.

Once again Mark pulled out his phone. This time, instead of calling Davis, he tried for Brodie. The guy answered on the second ring. "Brodie! Man, I was getting worried." Because this was not a good scene. "We think the stalker is on the ranch. He's been in the cottage, and he's—"

"What?" Brodie's voice was a roar. "Is Ava okay?"

"Yes." His gaze slanted toward her. "We wanted to make sure you, Jennifer and Davis were safe."

"I'm not at the ranch."

Mark heard Jennifer's voice in the background.

"We're in town, but we'll be there as fast as possible," Brodie continued.

Mac was heading toward the cottage's door.

"Is Davis with you?" Mark asked. His guts were knotting. This setup wasn't good. Every instinct he possessed was screaming *danger.*

"He's at the ranch."

Then why isn't he answering his phone?

"Protect my sister, Mark," Brodie said, his words rushing out. "Keep my family safe."

"Mac is here. We'll find out what's happening." He shoved the phone back into his pocket.

Mac was about to head into the cottage. "If he's here, he's not getting away—"

"I smell smoke," Ava said, her voice sharp and breaking with fear. "Don't you smell it?"

Mark's stables had been set on fire a few months ago, and he remembered the rush of fear he'd felt when he scented that smoke. Only the smoke had come with an explosion—one that had blasted right through the stables.

"Something is burning." Ava hurried away from the men. "It's coming from—*it's coming from the main house!*"

The main house... Was Davis there?

Mac ran and jumped into his truck. Ava and Mark pushed in with him. It wasn't far to the main house, and even as they drove up the lane, Mark was frantically trying to reach Davis on his phone again.

Then the truck came to a screeching halt. The ranch house was just feet away, and it was on fire.

The flames were flickering inside the house, rising in orange and red waves. Mark could see someone at the door, a man who appeared to be trying to break down the main entrance.

They all leapt from the truck and raced toward the house.

"Help me!" the man yelled. It was Sully. He was driving his shoulder into the door again and again. "It's stuck and I think Davis is inside!" But, then, before they could run to him, he turned and hurried toward the window in the front of the house. He lifted his hand and drove his fist straight into the glass.

Smoke billowed out as the glass shattered. Mark knocked as much glass out of the way as he could. Sully crawled through the window even as the crackle of the fire grew louder.

Mac headed in after him.

And Mark remembered another fire. The fire at his stables had been a trap. The man who'd set the blaze had been trying to get Jennifer. He'd set the fire to lure her out so he could grab her.

Mark swung around. Ava was right beside him. She pushed against him. "I need to get in there!"

But he caught her arms and held her back. "Mac and Sully will get Davis out."

Brodie's words rang in his mind. *Protect my sister.* That was exactly what he intended to do.

She struggled in his hold. "Mark, let me go!"

The flames were growing bigger. The scent of the fire was so much stronger. Mark needed to call 9-1-1. He had to—

A gunshot rang out. The blast was so close. Mark

could feel the heat of the bullet whipping by him before it plunged into the side of the house.

He yanked Ava forward, and they hit the ground.

SOMETHING WAS WRONG.

Davis tried to open his eyes, but that one small feat seemed to take way too much effort. His head was hurting, throbbing with a constant agony that had nausea rolling through him.

What happened?

He was on the floor, and he coughed because there was…smoke around him. His eyes cracked open, and he could see the tendrils of gray rising. His hands flattened on the wooden floor. Fire. That was right. He'd smelled smoke. He'd run out of his room and…

Did someone hit me? Because things were dark after that moment. He couldn't remember what had happened after he'd left his room.

He crawled forward, coughing more. He could hear the flames crackling and what sounded almost like laughter around him. Fire was racing up the walls, and he wanted to roar his fury. This was his home. He'd rebuilt it—he and Brodie had worked so hard to save this place.

Ava hated the ranch. She saw only pain there.

But it's my home. My life is here.

The flames grew bigger. Hotter.

"Davis!"

His head jerked when he heard the cry of his name. Through the smoke, he saw two dark figures surging toward him.

"Davis, are you all right?"

He would know that fierce, growling voice anyplace—

it was Sully's voice. And Sully was grabbing him, trying to help Davis get to the door.

"No, he's not all right," another sharp voice said. *Mac.* He slid his shoulder under Davis's right arm. "Come on, let's go!"

They half pulled, half carried him out of the hallway. The flames were racing across the den, moving so fast, and the sight of them made Davis's heart hurt. Not this place. It couldn't be destroyed. They needed it too much.

I need it.

They were close to the front door.

"That's why it wouldn't open," Sully said.

A table had been shoved against the door.

"Someone didn't want you getting out," Mac said.

Davis tried to speak but could only cough.

"Move that thing, Sully!" Mac ordered him. "Hurry!"

AVA STARED UP at Mark. He'd slammed into her and taken them both down to the ground. She knew he was trying to protect her from whoever was shooting at them.

The same man who set the house on fire.

"We have to help my brothers!" She pushed against Mark's shoulders.

But he didn't move. He wasn't moving!

"No, Ava, stop!" He caught her arms and pinned them in the dirt. "If we move, he'll have a perfect shot at us. That's what he planned, don't you see? This is a trap to lure us—*you*—out here. He's waiting for his moment to attack. The first shot missed, but the second? I don't think it will."

They were on the side of the house, low, hidden for the moment. But her brothers were in the fire. "Let me go," she told Mark, her voice sharp. She wasn't going to hide while her brothers died. *"Let me go!"* She bucked against him, heaving with all of her strength.

"Ava—"

Another shot rang out. Only this one…it hadn't been aimed at them. Mark's hold eased on her, and Ava twisted, rolling away from him. She stayed down, out of sight, but she saw that the bullet—and another one that had just blasted—had hit the front door of the ranch. A door that had opened just a few inches.

My brothers are trying to get out of the flames.

But whoever was out there—he was shooting at them. If her brothers ran out, he'd kill them. Ava knew this with utter certainty.

"No," she whispered as her heart splintered.

Mark's hands closed over her shoulders. "Stay here, baby, please," he told her, his voice so soft she barely heard his words. "I'll get them out. Just—*stay safe.*"

Then, before she could respond, Mark was up and running away. He was heading right for the front door, and he didn't have any weapon with him. "He's got a gun!" Mark bellowed. "Go out the back! Go!"

And gunfire erupted again.

"No!" Ava screamed. And she didn't stay there. She didn't hide.

She leaped to her feet.

"SOMEBODY IS SHOOTING at us!" Sully yelled as he held tighter to Davis.

They were at the front door. Mac had yanked open that door moments before, and air—clear, sweet air— had whispered inside. Davis choked and coughed because that clear air was gone, and the smoke was rising too fast.

The fire was burning all around them.

"He's got a gun! Go out the back! Go!"

Davis heard that frantic shout, and he looked over his shoulder. Flames were behind him. Where had all those flames come from? How had anyone gotten onto his ranch? *How?* The place should have been secure.

"We can't go back." Mac's voice was low and grim.

No, they couldn't.

"Let's head for a window. We'll break the glass, just like we did before," Sully said. And then Sully started pulling Davis toward the right.

In the next instant, Mac heard the thunder of gunfire. More bullets. Then—

"Stop!" Ava's scream, clear even above the flames. *"Leave them alone! If you want me, I'm here!"*

"No," Mac whispered.

Then the gunfire…it came again.

AVA LEAPT IN FRONT of Mark even as the gunfire exploded. She thought the bullets were going to slam into her. Mark was yelling and trying to push her behind him—

The bullets didn't hit her.

They slammed into the house.

Mark froze.

"He's not going to kill me," Ava said, her voice breaking. "He wants me alive, don't you see?" So he wouldn't shoot her. But if he had a shot at Mark, she didn't doubt for an instant that he'd take it. "If I'm here, he won't shoot."

And her brothers would have a chance. Because they *had* to get out of that fire. If they could just get out of the house and to the safety of Mac's truck or Sully's SUV, they'd make it.

"Hurry, Sully!" Ava called to her brother. The smoke was getting so thick out there. If it was bad on the narrow porch, what was it like in the house?

She risked a glance over her shoulder. Mark had finally let her go, and he'd shoved open the door to the house. He rushed inside—

And Ava stood there, her arms spread over her head, her feet braced apart. She was a target. She knew it. But more, she was a shield for her brothers and for Mark. For the men she loved so much.

Hurry.

"Come to me, Ava!" A hard, angry voice cried out from the darkness. "Come to me!"

She didn't move. Ava feared his words were just a trick. If she moved, then he would shoot.

"I'll kill them if you don't!" His voice was such a terrible roar.

"You'll kill them if I do." She wasn't budging and... yes, she could hear Mark behind her again. Mark and her brothers. They were coming out of the house. She moved then, but only so she could better shield them with her body.

He won't fire at me. He hasn't hurt me. He wants me alive. She just had to remember that.

"Ava!" Her name was a cry of absolute rage.

"Get to the vehicles," she told her brothers. They were low, crouching behind her. "Run!"

Run. Her father had said the same thing to her.

Despite the heat of the fire, Ava felt goose bumps rise on her arms.

"Move away from them!" the man in the darkness screamed.

But Ava wasn't about to abandon her brothers or Mark. So when they ran forward, she ran forward. She tried to stretch her arms and her body as much as possible to cover them.

"Ava!"

She flinched at that bellow of fury. And an instant later, gunfire erupted. But the bullet hit over her head, plunging into the wood of the porch.

Then another bullet hit about a foot away from her shoe.

Ava's breath sawed out and—*they were at the SUV.* They crouched behind it, and Ava reached for Davis. He was so still. When her fingers touched him, Davis flinched.

"Looks like the joker out there knocked Davis out," Sully said, "and then just left him to die in the fire."

A scream built in Ava's throat, but she choked it back.

"I'm calling 9-1-1," Sully declared.

Ava's fingers slid over Davis's jaw. "Are you okay?"

His hand lifted to curl tightly around hers. "Takes more than this...to stop me."

More than a fire? One that was destroying the home he'd worked so desperately to save? That house had been everything to Davis. She'd refused to set foot in the place, seeing only the pain there. But to him and Brodie, it had been so much more.

It had been...hope?

Now it was burning.

"I've got my weapon, and I'm going after him," Sully said. "Police and fire trucks are on the way."

But they'd get there too late for the house.

Mark had his phone out, too. "Bring every man and woman over here," Mark snapped into that phone. "We've got a fire at the McGuire ranch."

He put down the phone, then stared at Davis. "You and your family have always been there for me. Time for me to repay my debt."

Sully was already slipping away into the darkness. Ava wanted to grab him and hold on tight. The shooter out there wouldn't hesitate to fire at him.

But Sully—Sully was too fast. One instant he was there. The next he was gone.

Davis groaned. Mac leaned toward him. "You're bleeding so bad, man. What did he hit you with?"

And she could feel the blood streaming down his head. Davis. Her strong and tough brother. Another one who'd been hurt because he was trying to protect her.

"He'll get away," Ava said. Because if the guy had been good enough to sneak past their security, then he'd know a way off the property. Before help arrived, he'd be gone. "I have to stop him." This wasn't something she'd just leave to the others. Ava eased away from Davis. "Take care of him," she told Mac.

Mac was shaking his head. "Ava, whatever you're thinking—"

"I'm thinking that he won't shoot me, but he'll happily kill you all." This man was sick. And he was out there right then. "I'm going to draw him out."

"What?" Mark grabbed her arm. "No, baby, no!"

"Be ready," she told him as she straightened her spine. "I'll pull him out, and you get the bastard. Don't let him hurt anyone else." Then she leaned forward and kissed Mark. Fast, desperately. "Don't let him hurt you."

"Ava..."

She jerked away from him and ran. Not away from the ranch house, not this time. She wasn't going to leave those she loved behind, no matter the cost. Instead, she stood in front of the flames. Ava raised her hands high above her head. "I'm here!" she shouted. "If you want me... *I'm right here!* So come out and face me!"

AVA WAS CALLING to him, standing in front of those flames as they destroyed the house she hated. Did she realize he'd set the fire for her? To rid her of that terrible pain that she carried?

Her arms were open. She was yelling for him, and he wanted to turn and go to her so badly.

Ava. Sweet Ava. It had all been to prove his love to her. She didn't need Mark. She didn't need her brothers. She needed only him.

He heard the snap of a twig behind him.

He realized too late that he'd been hunted. His eyes had been on Ava, and he hadn't seen the threat closing in.

"Drop the weapon, you bastard," a low, guttural voice told him. "Or I will shoot you where you stand."

Slowly, never taking his eyes off Ava's form, he dropped the gun. It was one of the brothers who'd snuck up on him. The brothers had always been such an annoyance in his way, trying to block him from getting time with Ava.

Her parents had been in his way, but they'd been eliminated.

Now for her brothers...

"Take off the ski mask and turn to face me."

Taking his time, he lifted off the mask. He tossed it to the ground.

"Why the ski mask?" the brother demanded before he could turn to confront the fellow.

"Because I wanted to remind Ava." It was the truth. "I wanted her to remember that night whenever she looked at me."

"Did you kill our parents?" Ah, so much hate was in those words. He understood hate. Fury.

Fury could make a man careless.

Smiling, his hand slipped down to his waist. He had another weapon there, tucked in his waistband. His fingers curled around the gun. "I wish I had." He lifted it up and whirled in one movement. "Like I'm killing you!" He fired.

But—but the man had lurched to the side. Instead of hitting him in the chest, the bullet slammed into his prey's shoulder. And the man fired at him—a fast, rapid succession of shots.

One sank into his shoulder.

Another into his side.

No!

Pain tore through him, and he fired even as he staggered away. This wasn't supposed to happen. This wasn't the way things were supposed to end.

Not for him. Not for Ava.

Her brother stopped firing.

He ran for the sheltering darkness, even as the blood poured from his wounds.

Chapter Twelve

At the sound of the gunfire, Ava's breath caught in her throat. But those shots weren't aimed at her or the house or even at the SUV. They were coming from the west, from the line of trees just past the bluff.

"Sully," she whispered. Because he'd been out there, looking for the man who'd set that fire. If he'd found him— *"Sully!"*

And then she heard the growl of vehicles approaching. Lots of vehicles, from the sound of things. They were roaring up the drive, and all she could see was the bright flash of lights.

Then Mark was there, running to meet them. Shouting orders. She realized that help had come in the form of his workers and friends.

"We busted through the gate," she heard one man tell Mac. "Sorry about that, but the boss said we needed to get over here fast."

And they had. They were shining lights around the scene. Men were grabbing hoses and buckets of water and trying to put out the fire, trying to save the house.

A house she'd scorned for too long.

In the distance, Ava could hear a siren. An ambulance, coming to take care of Davis.

"Where's Sully?" Ava asked. Sullivan still hadn't appeared.

The men and women who'd arrived were fighting the flames, but no one was searching for Sully.

Ava started running toward the bluff.

Then she was grabbed from behind. Hard hands swung Ava around. "You're not going anyplace without me," Mark said.

She stared up at him, but a cloud had slid over the moon, and she couldn't see his face clearly. The scent of the fire was all around her, and so many memories were in the air. The past—the present—everything was tangling together.

Mark laced his fingers with hers. "Not without me," he said again.

He had a gun. She could see it in his other hand. Ava didn't even know where he'd gotten that weapon. From one of his men? From Mac?

But there was no time for questions. They ran toward the bluff. Mark's steps were sure, and she moved too fast to stumble. "Sully!" She cried out his name, but there was still no answer. She tried to keep her body in front of Mark's just in case the stalker was out there waiting for another shot, but Mark kept moving, trying to protect her.

When I want to keep him safe instead...

"Ava..." Her name was low, rough. And very close. She whirled to the left because she knew the sound of her brother's voice.

She and Mark leapt through the brush.

The clouds slid past the moon—

Sullivan was on the ground. He had a gun in his hand, and he was struggling to sit up. She ran to him and sank to her knees. "Sully!" When she touched him, she felt the sticky wetness of blood on him. So much blood.

"Shooting arm…went numb," he muttered. "Bullet's still in me…"

More than one bullet, judging by the amount of blood she felt. "Help!" Ava screamed, because the others back at the house had to be close enough to hear her. "Help—"

"No," Sully growled. "He's still here, Ava. He's close."

Mark swore. "Where?"

"Slid away to the…right…moving slow 'cause my bullets hit him, too…"

And Mark rushed to the right. Ava jumped up, wanting to follow him, but Sully had too tight a grip on her wrist. "Stay," he said. It wasn't an order but a plea. She didn't think tough Sully had ever pleaded for anything in his life.

Sully had been injured just a few months back. He'd gotten out of the hospital, supposedly with a clean bill of health, but…but he'd been taking fewer missions since then. And the way he was holding her hand so tightly…

She swallowed to clear the lump in her throat. "It's not just a bullet in your arm, is it? Were you shot somewhere else, too?"

"I…love you, Ava…"

Tears stung her eyes. No, no, this *wasn't* happening. Sully had survived so much. He was supposed to be invincible. He'd been her confidant for most of her life. The youngest brother, he'd been the closest to her age. The one who'd always taken the blame when she did ridiculous things because he'd said it was his job to keep her safe.

No matter what.

"Sully, *no.*" Her voice thickened. "Don't you do this to me. *Don't!*"

"Always hated…that I wasn't here when you needed me."

No, no, he was talking as if he were about to leave her. The final words of a dying man, and that couldn't happen. She *wouldn't* let it happen. "I'm going to get help. I'll be right back."

But he wasn't letting her go. His grip was so strong.

And tears were sliding down her cheeks.

"I'm sorry…" Sully told her. "I wanted…you safe…"

That too-tight grip went slack, and terror drove straight through her. "No!" Ava yelled. "No, no, Sully!" Her hands flew over his chest. And she'd been right. There were more wounds. His shirt was soaked with his blood. "Sully!" She wasn't even sure that he was breathing. She put her hands over those wounds, trying to apply as much pressure to them as she could. "Help me!" Ava screamed. But…but the fire was still raging. Would anyone hear her? Help was so close. She just had to run and get it.

"I'll be right back," Ava told him. She pressed a quick kiss to Sully's cheek. It was…chilled. No, *not Sully.* She staggered to her feet and turned to run back for help. Her shoes thudded over the earth as she hurried back toward the house and flames. As she ran faster, she could hear the horses screaming in the stable. The men were shouting and—

"Ava!"

She nearly ran into the shadowy form right before

her, but his hands flew out, and he grabbed her shoulders to steady her.

"Ava, what's happening? Are you hurt?" Ty demanded.

Ty. Right. He must have come with the group from Mark's ranch. "It's my brother," she said. "He needs help! Sully's been shot!"

The ambulance she'd heard was finally coming up the drive. She could see its shining lights.

"Take me to him," Ty ordered her. "Right now, Ava! Hurry!"

But Sully would need more than just Ty's help. They needed to get those EMTs to him. She tried to pull free. "I have to get to the ambulance—"

And something shoved into her side. Something cold, hard.

"You won't get to that ambulance," Ty told her, his words low and cutting. "And if you make one move to scream or try to fight me, I will shoot you where you stand."

That was a *gun* digging into her side.

Ty! Ty! Mark had been suspicious of him, but Ty had seemed to be so innocent. Oh, but he'd played that role far too well.

"You won't shoot me," Ava told him. Then she opened her mouth to scream.

His left hand slapped over her lips. "I will shoot you, and I will shoot every person who comes to your aid. I won't stop until there are no more bullets in this gun."

Over his shoulder, she could see the flames. The fire. Brodie had just arrived at the scene. Jennifer was with him.

"Do you want to see how many of them I can kill?"

Ava shook her head.

"Then you come with me, and you don't make a sound."

Brodie was looking at the house. He didn't see her. Ava swallowed, and then she nodded.

HE COULDN'T FIND the guy. Mark ran back through the brush, his gun clutched tightly in his hand. He hadn't wanted to get too far away from Ava. *But I wanted to find that bastard!*

He rushed back to her, but...

Ava wasn't there.

Sullivan was sprawled on the ground. Fear spiked in Mark's veins. "Sully!" He raced toward the man, but when he touched Sully, he knew the guy was in much worse shape than he'd originally realized. Sully's breath was barely whispering past his lips, and his skin was far too cold to the touch. "Sully, man, open your eyes. *Look at me!*" But Sully wasn't moving at all.

Mark glanced around, frantic. Where was Ava? She'd been there just a moment before.

I left her. I thought she was safe. I left her!

"Ava!" That wasn't his desperate call for her. Someone else was yelling out for her. Footsteps thudded toward him, and a flashlight shone in Mark's eyes. "What the... Mark?" The light dropped to the ground. *"Sully?"*

And then Brodie was running forward. Brodie's voice was a little harder and sharper than his twin's— that tone was a dead giveaway for his identity. Brodie yanked out his phone. Then he was saying, "I found Sully! West of the bluff, about fifty yards. Get the EMTs out here, now! He's hurt." His voice dropped and he added, "He's hurt bad."

Brodie tossed the phone aside. "Where's Ava?" he demanded.

"I don't know," Mark said, and the words actually hurt.

Brodie's head snapped up. "Where is my sister?"

Mark was already on his feet. *"Ava!"* He roared her name.

More footsteps thundered toward them. Help, coming for Sully.

But where was Ava?

Mark shouted her name again as he spun around. And fear—a dark terror unlike anything he'd ever known—tightened like a fist around his heart.

MARK WAS CALLING her name. Ava blinked, trying to stop her tears. He was so close—they were all so close. If she just called out to them—

"Mark will be the first to die," Ty promised her. "He can't hide behind you now."

"He was never hiding behind me."

"He wasn't worth your time. He was no good, a useless bastard who should never have touched you." He jerked her back against him, forcing her body even closer to his. "Knew you were meant for me…that very first night… I knew."

And he was dragging her back. Away from the lights. Away from her family. Away from Mark. Ava knew that if she didn't get away from him soon, there would be no escape.

"Thought they'd keep me from…you…" His breath rasped out. He was bleeding. She'd felt the blood as he held her so tightly to him. "No one can. Figured out how to slip in…and out of this ranch…"

He lived so close to the ranch. He'd had plenty of time to study the security system and find a flaw there. Her brothers had probably even talked with him about the system. After all, they'd thought Ty was a friend, just like Mark had.

They hadn't realized the secret side he'd been hiding. *I've known him for years.*

He stumbled a bit, and Ava used that moment to let her knees buckle. She slid down, acting as if she couldn't stop herself, and they both fell. The gun slid away from her body. The weapon slammed into the ground and discharged.

The bullet blasted, and Ava screamed. She screamed desperately—because she hoped that her brothers or Mark would hear her, and because that flying bullet had just sunk into her side. The pain was white-hot and burning. Like someone had shoved a fiery poker into her skin. Ty was on top of her, struggling to subdue her, but she was fighting him with all of her strength. Fighting and screaming and hoping—

Hear me over the fire. Hear the sound of that shot. Get to me!

Ty yanked Ava to her feet. He'd grabbed the gun again. "You shouldn't have done that… You'll *pay* for that, Ava."

And she knew…yes, she would pay.

Because he wasn't letting her go.

MARK'S HEAD WHIPPED to the right. A gunshot. He took off running even as Brodie shouted behind him. He shoved his way past the EMTs, and he kept bellowing Ava's name.

But he couldn't see her.

And the echo of that gunshot had already faded away.
No, no, he couldn't let her go.

I love you. Her words whispered through his mind.
He'd been stunned when she spoke those sweet words
to him. Ava...actually loving him? That was the only
dream he'd had. A dream so far-fetched that he'd never
dared voice it. When she'd said those words to him,
he'd been stunned.

And I didn't tell her how I felt. He'd been struck
dumb. So freaking happy, he'd been at a loss for the first
time in his life. He should have held her tight. Kissed
her deep and hard and told her that he loved her more
than anything. That she was the one thing that mattered
most in the world to him.

Ava. Always...Ava.

"Ava!" Mark yelled. *"Where are you?"*

And if he lost her, Mark knew nothing else would
ever matter to him again.

THE EMTs WERE forcing Davis into the back of an ambulance. He didn't want to go. Ava was missing! He
needed to search for her. He needed—

"Get in," Jennifer told him flatly. "Before you pass
out."

And then he saw Sully being loaded into the same
ambulance. Only Sully looked bad. Scary bad. His
skin was ashen, and the bright lights in the ambulance
showed the blood that was pouring from his wounds.

"No," Davis gritted out. This couldn't be happening again. He tried to go to Sully, but the EMTs shoved
him back.

"Mark hasn't found her."

His head snapped up at Brodie's words. His twin

stood at the back of the ambulance, fear stamped on his face. Jennifer reached for him, curling her hand around his arm.

"He's searching—running around like mad, but she's vanished." Fear cracked in those words. "I called Grant. He's coming...*but she's gone.*"

Rage was giving Davis the strength to stay upright. His head still pounded as if a sledgehammer was shoving against his skull, but he had to say this... "Alan... Channing..." The stalker had to be that jerk. "He...took... her..." If they could get an APB out on the guy, then they could track him. They could find Ava. They could—

"No..." That weak rasp came from Sully.

Davis looked over at him. Sully's hand had risen and locked around the wrist of the EMT. The guy held a syringe in his fingers, but Sully was stopping the him. He was saying— "I...saw him... Not Ch-Channing... Tell Mark...it was...Ty..."

Ty?

Davis shook his head.

When he looked back out of the ambulance, he saw that Brodie had already whirled away. The guy was running for the cops.

Another EMT started to slam those doors shut. Davis lurched forward and out of the ambulance before they could close him inside. He nearly fell on his face, but Jennifer helped to catch him. Davis looked back at the stunned EMTs. "Take...care of my brother..." Davis said.

Because he was going to help his sister.

MARK RAN INTO the stables at the McGuire ranch. The horses were crying out, no doubt scared by the flames and the smoke. He rushed through the stalls, stopping only when he neared Lady.

Ava's horse. A beauty who wasn't shaking like the others. She came toward him, lowering her head. He reached out to her. "Help me find her." Because he could cover so much more ground on that horse's back.

In moments, he had her saddled up and ready to go. He urged the mount forward, and Lady galloped out of the stables. He could barely breathe because fear was clawing into his chest. Ava's image flashed in his mind. She'd been so determined to protect him and her brothers and so sure that the stalker wouldn't shoot her...

I hope she's right. Please, God, let her be right. Maybe the stalker wasn't hurting her. If Mark could just get to her in time...

"Mark!" Brodie ran toward him. "It's Ty! He's the one who took Ava! Sully told us...it was him!"

The fury within Mark coalesced, seeming to freeze his heart with an icy fire. He went numb then, operating on pure, cold instinct.

Brodie's breath heaved out. "Where would he take her?"

Someplace close. Someplace where he could hide her. Maybe he thought Sully was dead. Maybe Ty thought no one knew that *he* was the one who'd attacked that night.

"The security system is back up and running," Brodie said. "It looks like he slipped in via the south gate."

The south gate. The gate that was closest to Mark's property.

"Then that's how he's going to try to get out." Mark urged the horse onward. "I'll get her back," he shouted to Brodie. Brodie was running into the stables, too, and so was…Davis? Staggering, yes, but still trying to follow his twin.

Mark leaned low over the horse's mane. He urged Lady to go faster. To run harder.

Years ago, Ava had made that same desperate night journey with Lady. She'd gotten to him safely, and now Mark was frantic to get to her.

I'm coming, Ava. I'm coming.

TY WAS DRAGGING AVA, pulling her and trying to force her to run, but every step was agony for her. She was sure the bullet was still inside her. She hadn't felt it come out, and the pain wrenched through her.

"We'll get clear of the McGuire ranch, and then I'll take you away," he said. He'd been talking to her, muttering constantly, as he hauled her through the darkness. "It'll be just you and me, Ava. The way it should have been. Then I'll get rid of Mark, and everything— *everything will all be mine.*"

He was insane. Straight-up certifiable.

Ava slipped and fell, but this time, the stumble wasn't a fake-out designed to gain her freedom. Her legs just wouldn't go anymore, and she hit the ground.

"Get up!" Ty screamed at her.

Ava tried, but she couldn't.

"Get up!" He grabbed her hair, jerked her head back and put the gun in her face. "Or I will shoot you!"

She stared up at him. "You…already did."

"Wh-what?" And there was fear in that one word. He'd hurt so many people—and yet he sounded terrified in that moment. "When?" His hand flew over her, and when he touched her wound, Ava hissed out a breath. *"No!"* Ty bellowed.

No? He was the one screaming as if he were in agony, but she had the bullet in her side.

He hauled her to her feet. "You'll be okay." Was he saying that to convince her or himself? "Bullets grazed me, too. I'm still going…" The words came faster. *Faster.* "You'll be okay…"

"Didn't…graze me." She swallowed, trying to clear the thick lump in her throat. "It's…in me." She sagged to her knees before him.

He froze. "I didn't mean to hurt you." The words were low and hoarse and so absolutely insane that she had to bite back the hysterical laughter that rose to her lips. "You shouldn't have fought me. You should have just come with me."

And he shouldn't have tried to kill her brother. Or set fire to her family home. Or terrorized her for so long.

Ava stared up at him. The moon was behind Ty. Big and full and bright. "Why?" She just didn't understand. "Why…me?"

His hand stroked over her cheek. "Because you're just like her."

She shook her head, not understanding.

"He was obsessed with her, and I'm… I'm consumed by you."

Her body shuddered.

"He couldn't have her, and it drove the old man crazy. I'll prove that I'm better than he ever was. I'll have you."

The old man… Understanding clicked for her. "Gregory? Gregory Montgomery?" He'd been—wait, he'd dated her mother but—

"He wanted her, always her. My mother wasn't good enough. He treated her like garbage." His fingers slid down her jaw. Tightened. Bruised. "He hurt her. Again and again…because she wasn't the woman he wanted."

Gregory had been involved with Ty's mother?

"I'll have you…you're the one I want. Mark thinks you're his, but he's wrong. He got everything else. Even though he wasn't the bastard's real son. *Everything else*, but he won't get you."

She heard the thunder of approaching horse hooves pounding across the earth.

"That's him," Ty said. He uttered those words with such certainty, and when his head moved just a little bit, she realized he was smiling. "He thinks he's coming to the rescue. He doesn't know that I've planned for him to die all along."

Ava shook her head. "Please don't."

"Don't beg for him!" His fingers were so tight she feared he'd break her jaw. "He's nothing! He got *my* life, and he should have been tossed into the streets years ago!" His voice was cracking. "Then he locked his sights on you. He wanted you… I knew it… Mark wanted you more than anything. More than *my* ranch. More than the life that was *mine*. And I wasn't going to let him have you. I was going to show him—the thing he wanted most was *mine*!"

The horse and its rider were getting closer. And Ty was still right in front of her with his gun. Ava gathered her strength. She wasn't going to let Mark die. Any pain, any sacrifice, would be worth his life.

"You can watch him die," Ty told her. He said the words as if he were offering her some kind of gift. Maybe in his messed-up mind, he was. "Then you'll know…it will just be you and me. Forever."

No, it wouldn't be.

"Ava!" That was Mark's voice. So strong. So fierce. He'd spotted them. Did he see Ty's gun? *"Get away from her!"*

But Ty just slid closer to her. "Watch closely," he told Ava. "Sully didn't see my weapon, either, not until it was too late."

Sully. She pressed her lips together to stop their trembling. She wasn't going to watch anything—especially not Mark's death. "You said…you didn't mean to shoot me."

"I don't want to hurt you," he whispered.

She tipped her head back even more. Could he see her smile as clearly as she'd seen his? "Guess what? I *do* want to hurt you." Then Ava surged up. She ignored the pain of her wound. She pushed her fear away. And she hit him. Ava slammed into him with all of her might. Her head hit his nose, and Ava was sure she heard the crack of his nose breaking. He howled and tried to strike out at her.

The gun was coming close to her, but he was falling back. Falling—and crashing into the ground. Ava leapt away from him and started running toward Mark. "Go back!" Ava screamed. "He's got a gun! Go back!"

Mark was racing forward on the horse.

Her legs were shaking and—

"Down, Ava! Down!" Mark's wrenching cry.

Ava fell.

And Mark—Mark fired the gun he held. *Boom. Boom.* Her hands pushed against the earth, and she glanced over her shoulder. Ty was on his feet, the gun in his hand. Had he been about to shoot her? Or Mark?

As she stared at him, Ty staggered. The gun fell

from his fingers, and his knees hit the ground. "You... were...mine..."

Ava shook her head. "No, you bastard. I wasn't." She rose, slowly, her hand pressed to her side. She could feel the blood spilling through her fingers. Lady neighed behind her, but Ava didn't look back. She was afraid to take her eyes off Ty. Afraid that he'd be like one of those horrible movie monsters that just rose again and again and kept attacking until everyone else was dead.

"Ava!" Mark was there, wrapping his arms around her and holding her tight. She still didn't look away from Ty. He was sprawled on the ground now, his body heaving. He'd hurt so many people.

"I was afraid I wouldn't get to you in time," Mark rasped. He pressed a kiss to her cheek. "I think I lost about fifty years of my life when I was racing on Lady."

She wanted to look at him. She needed to hold him.

But her body had frozen. "He's not dead," she told Mark. Her voice sounded too husky. As if she'd been screaming for hours, but she hadn't. Her knees had locked so that she wouldn't fall. She didn't feel cold any longer, and her wound didn't ache. She didn't feel the wound at all.

More hoofbeats thundered toward them.

Mark pulled Ava back. His touch was so careful and gentle. He didn't know just how much Ty hated him. Not yet. Ava found herself easing over, trying to stand in front of Mark.

"No." Now his voice was hard. "Don't ever risk your life for me again."

"I love you." Again, her words were too soft. "It's what I do." You protected those you loved. It was a Mc-Guire rule.

Brodie ran past Mark, heading toward the prone figure of Ty.

Mark stepped in front of Ava, finally blocking her view of the fallen man. "Ava, please, look at me."

Her gaze rose to his face. The moon shone down on them.

"I love you," he said, his voice strong and clear. "And that's what I do."

A sob built in her throat, but she wouldn't let the sound escape.

"I would risk my life for you in an instant. I would kill for you. Baby, I would do anything for you." His lips came down and touched hers. "Because you are the one thing in this world that I cannot live without."

And she didn't want to live without him.

The kiss was bittersweet, and the ice around her began to melt as he held her close. Mark—he was safe. Brodie was safe. Ty—

"He's still alive," Brodie snarled.

Mark pulled her close. He turned his body as he glanced over at Brodie, and Ava saw her brother's hands fist in Ty's shirt as he yanked the other man up to a sitting position and cursed. Brodie's voice was a low, lethal drawl. "You are going to rot in prison for what you've done to my family!"

Ty laughed. "You...need me. I...know."

"What do you know?" Brodie shook him. "You're a psycho who doesn't even—"

"I know...who killed them."

Ava's heart slammed into her chest. Her fingers pressed harder to her wound. She still didn't feel the pain. What had happened to the pain?

"I was...watching Ava. Saw them."

She shook her head. No, no, he'd been at the Montgomery ranch when she rushed over there that night—right? But when she tried, Ava couldn't remember seeing him that long-ago night. She'd just seen Mark when she arrived at the ranch. He'd sent out his men. She'd assumed Ty had been sent then, too.

"You…need me." And Ty kept laughing.

Davis advanced from the darkness. His steps were slow, cautious. Davis wasn't the cautious type. She reached out to him.

"Ava…" He pulled her away from Mark and into his arms. He whispered a confession in her ear. "You scared me."

She squeezed her eyes shut. She could hear Brodie talking to someone—he was barking orders and demanding the cops rush over, so she figured he had to be on his phone. Mark was close, right at her back. And Davis was holding her so tightly that she could barely pull in a breath.

Davis and Mark had been afraid they'd lose her. She'd been afraid they'd be hurt. But they'd all made it out of that mess alive.

Mark loves me. He'd said she mattered more than anything to him. There was too much fear still swirling in her heart for his words to sink in, but they would—she knew they would. Then she'd be happy. This nightmare would finally be over.

"Sully?" She had to force out his name. For some reason, it was getting harder to talk.

"On the way to the hospital," Davis quickly told her. "He's alive, Ava. And he's a fighter. All the McGuires are. You know that."

Yes, they were fighters.

Davis let her go, and Ava started to fall. She just didn't have the strength to stand any longer. She expected to hit the ground and she couldn't even brace for the impact, but Mark caught her. His arms wrapped around her as he cradled her so carefully. As if she were precious to him.

I love him. Probably more than he'd ever realize. Enough to trade her life for his without any hesitation.

"Baby?" His hold tightened on her. "Ava? Ava, what's wrong?"

She heard Ty's laughter again. Wild. Cruel.

"You won't have…her!" Ty promised. "She's gone… you lost her…you lost!"

Mark's hand pressed over her wound. Ava's breath hissed out, and he looked down at her side.

"No," he said, voice gone hoarse with horror. "Ava, *no!*"

She licked her lips. They were so dry. And the pain had come back.

Mark was on his feet and running with her cradled in his arms. "I'll get the EMTs! You'll be fine, you'll be—"

"I love you," she told him, needing to say those words once again. Her eyelids were sagging closed. "And…don't worry…"

"Ava!"

"You heard…Davis… McGuires are…fighters…" She would fight for him—for their chance at a life together—with every bit of strength she had.

He loved her. She loved him. And Ty *didn't* get to win.

Ava didn't open her eyes. Not yet. She knew she was in a hospital. She remembered the frantic ambulance ride there. The way Mark had clung so tightly to her hand. The way he'd said—

I love you.

Over and over again.

The bullet had been taken out. She'd been stitched up. Things were really foggy after that point.

She expected pain. But…there wasn't any. Just a heavy lethargy that seemed to weigh down her body.

"Mark." She whispered his name because he was the first person she thought about. The one she needed most.

Warm fingers curled around her hand. "I'm right here."

She opened her eyes. He was beside her. Stubble lined his jaw, and dark shadows swept under his eyes.

"Right here," he said, "with you. The one place I always want to be."

Happiness spread within her. They'd made it. They'd— "Sully?"

"Right here, sis," said a low voice. She turned her head to the left. There was another bed in that hospital room. Sully was there, looking tired but still managing to smile. "You know I'm hard to kill."

Her breath heaved out in a sound that was a cross between a sob and a laugh. Yes, he was hard to kill. He was a fighter.

A McGuire.

And they'd won.

Mark's fingers swept back her hair. His touch seemed to sink right through her. "I want to date you, Ava."

His words—after everything that had occurred— had her shaking her head. "What?"

"I want to date you, properly. The flowers and the

dinners and anything and everything you want." He swallowed, cleared his throat. "And when you're ready, I want to marry you. If you'll have me."

If?

"Because I do love you, and I'd like to spend the rest of my life making you happy."

Her lips parted.

"Aw, man, Ava, I should've gotten my own room!" Sully groaned.

She ignored him and focused on Mark. "You don't need to date me."

Worry flashed in his eyes.

"But you do need to marry me." They'd been through hell together, and they'd come out stronger for it. "Because I don't want to spend any more days or nights without you."

A wide smile spread across his face.

"Definitely my own room," Sully muttered.

Mark leaned forward. "I love you."

And Ava knew that the nightmare was over. Finally, everything was going to be all right.

Epilogue

Mark walked into the small interrogation room at the Austin Police Department. Davis was right at his heels. He didn't know what kind of strings Davis had pulled in order to get this little one-on-one chat, but Mark figured he'd owe his brother-in-law-to-be for this one.

Ty glared at him. His ex-foreman and friend was handcuffed to the little table. He wore a garish orange prison uniform, and hate burned in his eyes.

Mark stared at him a moment as the past swam in front of him. Those brown eyes...filled with burning hate...he'd seen them before.

Eyes in another man's face. The same hate reflected in a gaze just as dark.

"You're his son," Mark said. Because he'd put all the puzzle pieces together after he talked with Ava and Davis. "Gregory Montgomery's son."

"His *real* son!" Ty shouted. He tried to surge forward, but the handcuffs yanked him right back down. "You were nothing to the old man, but he still left you everything! He gave you everything!"

And he had. Gregory Montgomery's will had stipulated that all of his holdings were to pass directly to Mark. There'd even been some legal mumbo jumbo about no additional heirs—even biological offspring—ever being able to claim his assets. At the time, Mark hadn't paid any attention to that clause, but now...*it makes sense.* "He knew about you."

"He never thought I was good enough!" That hate just burned hotter in his stare. "Never thought my mom was good enough. But I showed him!"

Davis propped his shoulders against the wall on the right. "Just so you know," Davis murmured, "you're being watched and recorded."

Ty's gaze slanted toward the one-way mirror. "You think I care?"

He should. He was about to talk away any chance he had at ever seeing the outside of a prison.

"I've been robbed my whole life, and I'm *glad* to tell the world now." His chin jutted up. "That old bastard? The one you let punch you around? I'm the one who was strong enough to stand up to him. *I* killed him."

Mark had already suspected as much.

"Then I found out about that bull he'd put in his will. He'd told me—weeks before!—that I was gonna get what I had coming to me. He *lied*!"

"No." Mark shook his head. "He gave you exactly what he wanted you to have."

Nothing.

Gregory had always been a twisted bastard.

Davis pushed away from the wall and headed toward the table.

"I was gonna show him," Ty said, his words coming out so fast and hard. "I was gonna take Ava...he couldn't get her mother, but I would get her. Ava was even prettier. She was perfect. She was—"

Davis slammed his hands down on the table in front of Ty. Ty flinched.

"If you say that my sister was going to be yours," Davis told him, "then I will slam my fist into your face and break your nose again."

Because Ava had broken his nose the night of the fire, and Mark's bullets had kept the man in the hospital for over a week.

"Do you think I had it easy?" Mark asked him, curious now. "You know what he did to me."

Ty's lips twisted. "I guess you've never seen my back. He did the same thing to *me.*

"You won't let me go to prison." Ty leaned forward. He seemed cocky now. So confident. "You'll make a deal for me." He inclined his head toward Davis. "Because if you do, then I'll tell you what I saw that night. I'll tell you who killed your parents."

Silence.

Then...

"You attacked my sister," Davis said. His voice was low and cutting. "I don't care what you know. You're going to rot in jail." He looked back at Mark. "I think we've got everything we need. The cops heard him confess to killing Gregory. They already had him dead to rights on the other attacks. He's done."

Then he turned his back and walked away.

"No," Ty whispered. "No!" He tried to shoot to his feet, but once more, the handcuffs just pulled him back.

Mark stared at him. He wanted to hurt the man. To destroy him the same way Ty had tried to destroy everything Mark held dear, but...

Ava was waiting for him. *Life* was waiting.

"Goodbye, Ty." They'd gotten the confession that the cops needed.

Ty was screaming when they left him.

THE RANCH HOUSE had been saved. Mark figured that was pretty much a miracle. His men and the firefighters had been able to contain the blaze. The den, Davis's bedroom and the hallway were charred, but the structure of the place was fairly intact. The home could be repaired. Rebuilt.

"How much pain," Davis asked quietly as he gazed at the house, "do you think one place can stand? How much...before you just have to walk away?"

Mark put his hand on his friend's shoulder. "Ava is here."

Davis's head whipped toward him.

"She's on the bluff."

Davis shook his head. "Ava...doesn't like this place."

Mark just stood quietly with his friend.

A few moments later, Ava joined them. Davis stared at her as if she were a ghost.

"I have some ideas," Ava said as she cocked her head and studied the house. "About how we can repair this place."

"You...you want to rebuild?" Davis's voice was strangled.

Ava nodded. Her left hand reached for Mark's. Their fingers threaded together. "Yes. After all...it's home."

Davis was still as stone.

Ava's right hand reached out to him. Her fingers threaded with his, too. "Home is important," she told Davis. "So is family."

"Nothing's more important than family," Davis agreed, his words a rough rasp.

Ava smiled at him, she winked at Mark and then she looked at the house once more. "I have some ideas..." she said again.

A few minutes later, Ava climbed into the car. They were about to head back to Mark's ranch, and he couldn't wait to get her back there and into his bed. But first...

Mark looked over at Davis. "You know you aren't going to let things end this way."

Davis was staring at the house. "Ava wants to rebuild." He sounded dazed.

Mark shook his head. "That's not what I'm talking about."

Davis turned to face him.

"If Ty knows who killed your parents, we have to make him talk."

Davis smiled then, and the sight was chilling. "Oh, don't worry, he'll talk." His eyes glinted. "I've already put plans in motion."

A cold chill slid up Mark's spine.

"I *will* find out who killed my parents. Before I'm done, Ty Watts will be begging to tell me everything he knows."

Staring into Davis's cold gaze, Mark believed him. But then, he knew just how deadly Davis McGuire truly was. "If you need me," Mark told him, "you know where I'll be."

Davis nodded. "With my sister...protecting her with your life."

"Always," Mark promised him. Then he turned and headed toward the car—and Ava.

DAVIS WATCHED AVA and Mark pull away. Mark loved Ava. Of that, Davis had no doubt. Ava was happy, safe.

And now—now he could focus on the past once again. Every day he felt as if he learned a new piece of the puzzle that was his parents' murder. Every day he got closer to the truth.

Yes, Ty would talk…sooner or later.

The guilty would be found. Davis wasn't going to rest until he gave his parents the justice they deserved.

McGuires were fighters, and he still had plenty of fight left within him.

* * * * *

SPECIAL EXCERPT FROM

HARLEQUIN®

INTRIGUE

Read on for a sneak preview of
HIGH COUNTRY HIDEOUT, the next installment of
COVERT COWBOYS, INC.
by New York Times *bestselling author*
Elle James

Ranching was Angus Ketchum's first love—until
his last tour of duty shattered that dream. The wounded
ex-soldier gets his second chance when he's recruited
to go undercover to protect widowed ranch owner
Reggie Davis.

Angus slipped through the wooden rails and waded through the cattle milling around, waiting for the gate to open with the promise of being fed on the other side.

The rider nudged his horse toward the gate and leaned down to open it. Apparently the latch stuck and refused to open. Still too far back to reach the gate first, Angus continued forward, frustrated at his slow pace.

As the horseman swung his leg over to dismount, the gelding screamed, reared and backed away so fast the rider lost his balance and fell backward into the herd of cattle.

Spooked by the horse's distress, the cattle bellowed and churned in place, too tightly packed to figure a way out of the corner they were in.

The horse reared again. Its front hooves pawed at the air then crashed to the ground.

Unable to see the downed cowboy, Angus pushed forward, slapping at the cattle, shoving them apart to make a path through their warm bodies.

Afraid the rider would be trampled by the horse or the cattle, Angus doubled his efforts. By the time he reached him, the cowboy had pushed to his feet.

The horse chose that moment to rear again, his hooves directly over the rider.

Angus broke through the herd and threw himself into the cowboy, sending them both flying toward the fence, out of striking distance of the horse's hooves and the panicking cattle.

Thankfully the ground was a soft layer of mud to cushion their landing, but the cowboy beneath Angus definitely took the full force of the fall, crushed beneath Angus's six-foot-three frame.

Immediately he rolled off the horseman. "Are you okay?"

Dusk had settled in, making it hard to see.

Angus grabbed the man's shoulder and rolled him over, his fingers brushing against the soft swell of flesh beneath the jacket he wore. His hat fell off and a cascade of sandy-blond hair spilled from beneath. Blue eyes glared up at him.

The cowboy was no boy, but a woman, with curves in all the right places and an angry scowl adding to the mess of her muddy but beautiful face. "Who the hell are you, and what are you doing on my ranch?"

Don't miss HIGH COUNTRY HIDEOUT
by New York Times *bestselling author Elle James,*
available October 2015 wherever
Harlequin Intrigue® books and ebooks are sold.

www.Harlequin.com

Love the Harlequin book you just read?

Your opinion matters.

Review this book on your favorite
book site, review site, blog or your own
social media properties and share
your opinion with other readers!

Harlequin has everything from contemporary, passionate and heartwarming to suspenseful and inspirational stories.

Whatever your mood, we have a romance just for you!

Connect with us to find your next great read, special offers and more.

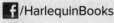

/HarlequinBooks

@HarlequinBooks

www.HarlequinBlog.com

www.Harlequin.com/Newsletters

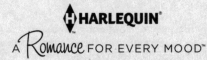

HARLEQUIN®

A *Romance* FOR EVERY MOOD™

www.Harlequin.com